To Harley
  I hope you enjoy
this book.

TIGER, TIGER

Galaxy Craze

Also by Galaxy Craze

By the Shore

Galaxy Craze

TIGER, TIGER

Black Cat
New York
a paperback original imprint of Grove/Atlantic, Inc.

Published simultaneously in Canada
Printed in the United States of America

FIRST EDITION

ISBN-10: 0-8021-7054-4
ISBN-13: 978-0-8021-7054-5

Black Cat
a paperback original imprint of Grove/Atlantic, Inc.
841 Broadway
New York, NY 10003

Distributed by Publishers Group West

www.groveatlantic.com

08 09 10 11 12   10 9 8 7 6 5 4 3 2 1

For Sam
with love and respect

Tiger, Tiger

ONE

The last time my mother left my father, he was sitting at the kitchen table. "Simon," she said, "I'm leaving you." She stood by the front door with her winter coat on, holding Eden's hand. I stood beside them, looking down the hallway to the kitchen.

He stared at the cup of tea in front of him. Our mother turned the door handle and he looked up suddenly, as though startled by the sound of the latch. He sat at the table watching us leave, his mouth slightly open.

"Come on, May," my mother said, as I lingered in the doorway. I thought, I should look back; I should say good-bye to him. But when she called my name again, I followed her down the front steps.

She walked quickly down the street, her coat open and her breath visible in the cold morning air. In the fluster and rush, her handbag slipped from her shoulder and she stumbled on the pavement. "Hurry," she said, as though we were running for a train, as though someone were chasing us in the dark. It was Sunday morning, the street was empty and quiet, and our car was parked at the end of the road.

I thought, Soon we'll hear his footsteps running up behind us. *Lucy, wait . . . stop! Don't leave. What are you doing?* But there were none.

While we sat in the car, waiting for the engine to warm, the front door of our house remained closed. With one hand on the steering wheel, my mother bit her thumbnail. "He couldn't even be bothered to get up from the table and say good-bye," she said. "He was probably worried his tea would get cold."

The lorries sped by on the motorway. Water splashed from the wheels as they drove through puddles left over from last night's rain. Eden sat in the backseat, looking out the rear window. Mum glanced at him as she drove. "Are you all right back there?"

There was a nervous, quick sound in her voice. Eden turned away from the window. He looked as though he had just woken from a dream.

"All right, my darling?" she said, with a worried smile.

On the misted passenger-side window, I drew a simple house, a tree—then wiped it away with my sweater sleeve. Mum sighed, staring ahead at the road as she drove. Her mascara had fallen beneath her eyes, leaving dark shadows. She reached forward, turning the dial on the radio, but the stations came in filled with static and reports of rain.

In the shopping bag by my feet, she had packed sandwiches and a packet of digestive biscuits. Eden lay down under an old fur coat on the backseat. The leaves on the trees by the side of the road shone wet and green.

We stopped for lunch in Penrith in a village with a wishing well in the center. We drove through Carlisle and stopped at the Little Chef near Hadrian's Wall for a strawberry milk and ice lolly.

In Dunblane, we turned off the motorway, driving slowly along the streets of town and up a dirt road to a whitewashed house made of stone. My grandfather's house had a name: Caldhame.

Mum turned the engine off. She studied her reflection in the rearview mirror. She pulled out a crumpled tissue from her bag, spat on it, and tried to wipe the mascara from beneath her eyes.

Eden opened the car door. The cold air rushed inside to greet us. After the long drive, it did not feel like a relief to have finally arrived. Outside, I brushed the biscuit crumbs from my skirt, and they disappeared into the gravel road.

Grandfather came from the house in his raincoat and boots, his walking stick in his hand. He was a tall man, his hair almost white. He waved, smiling at us. We were hours late; the rain had been hard, the telephone at the rest station broken. His two dogs, black pugs, ran and leapt around us.

"Hello, Father," our mother said, as she leaned toward him, kissing him on his cheek. "You look well."

Eden gave Grandfather a hug. After a moment of looking awkward, unsure of where to put his arms, Grandfather patted Eden on the back. Eden let go, causing Grandfather to step backward, stumbling slightly. He watched Eden as he ran to the dogs, kneeling in the wet grass to play with them.

"I wouldn't if I were you," Grandfather called out to him. "They've just rolled in the remains of a dead bird."

Eden didn't hear—or didn't care—that the dogs smelled of dead bird. He lay down on the ground, encouraging them to jump all over him.

"Hello, young lady."

"Hello, Grandfather." My voice, a curtsy.

The air was cool and blowing sideways.

Grandfather took off his hat and held it in his hands. As a young man, he had fought in the war. He flew Mosquitoes and Spitfires in the Royal Air Force. When the war ended and he came home, one of the few survivors of the RAF, he was told that his two brothers had been killed. Grandfather had a fallen look in his eyes, even when he laughed and smiled, as though he had only recently heard the news of their deaths.

Inside the house, Mrs. Stirling, the daily, was boiling water for tea. Her cheeks were round and flushed. "Had a long journey? Terrible weather, isn't it. The sufferings for our sins. Anyway, at least there's tea on the table."

And there *was* tea on the table! Oaten biscuits on a plate, blue cheese, butter, scones, and blackberry jam. Even a yellow and chocolate layer cake. My stomach rumbled as I looked at the food, deciding what to try first.

At the table, our mother told Grandfather how well the furniture shop was doing. Lulu, a famous singer, had come in just the other day and spent over two hundred pounds, and *Tatler* was doing a write-up!

"Not one of those awful pop singers?" Mrs. Stirling said.

"No," Mum said, a bite of scone crumbling into her cupped hand. "I think you would like her voice."

When she spoke about the shop, she spoke in a glossy, busy voice, as though she were dressed in a black suit, with straightened hair and red lipstick. Her hands flickered in the air; the small stone in her ring sparkled.

"I'm glad to hear it," Grandfather said. "Things are coming together for you two finally."

Then suddenly, as though exhausted by herself—the quick voice, the black suit, the sparkle on her ring too small to flame— our mother froze. She stopped speaking and looked up from the crumbs on her plate, from Grandfather to Eden to me, as though searching for someone to hold.

Grandfather looked at her in a peculiar way, as though he could not understand this change. "Lucy? Darling, whatever is the matter?"

Mum blew her nose into her napkin. She shook her head. "Nothing. Nothing's the matter."

Eden stared across the table at our mother crying into a napkin. A piece of yellow and chocolate layer cake lay half eaten on his plate. She wiped her eyes dry, but her voice shook when she spoke. "Oh, I'm sorry. I'm just tired, I think; that's all." She waved her hand in the air, as though trying to erase what had just happened. As though to say, Let's start over again.

She straightened herself in the chair.

"So, how have you been, Father?"

"Oh, fine, fine." Like the chime of a clock. He had never liked to talk about himself. "I sold the south field to the farmer down the road. He needed it for his sheep."

Mum nodded, twisting the tissue in her hand. Over the years he had sold off parcels of land, cutting them away like pieces of a cake. He had left his position at the bank and was a pensioner now, with a small added income from the outbuildings and the land he let.

"Is everything all right with you and Simon?" Grandfather asked cautiously, knowing this was usually the reason for our sudden visits.

Mum shook her head. "It's never all right for long." Grandfather reached for the handle of his teacup. He was a man, our mother had told us, who wanted peace in his life. The flat line of the green fields. His ex-wife, my mother's mother, Anne, was restless like my mother. She had grown bored with marriage, motherhood, and Scotland and left him for an American businessman. Our mother was only eight when her mother left her.

Lucy, Grandfather said, was like her mother. She could never settle into one place. Like a clock, always ticking with a low hum of dissatisfaction. Always looking for something else, something more, somewhere over there. Our mother wanted so much from the world, of love and happiness and other invisible things with wings.

"We had a row last night," our mother said. "On the street in front of the house. I'm afraid all the neighbors must have heard. At least I won't have to face them today."

"What about?" Grandfather asked.

"Oh, it's so stupid." She pressed her fingertips to her forehead. "We went out to a party, and on the way home I realized I had lost one of the earrings he'd given me for my birthday. I was sure it had fallen off on the street, because I remembered having them on when we left the party. So we went back to search for it, and he gets all upset, telling me I don't look out for the things I have . . . and this means I don't really care. . . ." Her voice faded, as though the ending would be written in the air.

I knew the earring she had lost. Our father had carried the stones back from Morocco in a tissue in his jeans pocket.

"So," she continued, "I tried to tell him he shouldn't get so upset over material things. It was just an earring. Well, he starts telling me I'm spoiled because I grew up not worrying about money . . . the usual crap."

Grandfather looked at his hands on the table. His skin had become transparent with age. The dark blue veins, his wrist bones close to the skin. When he grew older, I thought, you would see inside of him.

"Why didn't you just apologize? Say you were sorry for losing the earring?"

Mum brought her hand to her chest, shocked by the suggestion. "Me, apologize? What for?"

Grandfather frowned.

"Why should I apologize? Earrings get lost all the time, every minute of the day." She shut her mouth quickly, as though trying to keep the next word in. "Actually, I was so furious I took off the other earring and threw it down the rain gutter."

"Lucy!" Grandfather said.

"Mum," I said.

She stared back at us. Her eyes shone, as though they were saying, Yes, I did it! I threw the earring down the rain gutter.

"Lucy." Grandfather sighed. "Why do you behave so childishly? So foolishly. Simon is your husband. Don't you want to have a nice life together instead of all this fighting?"

There was a time, at the beginning of their romance, when Grandfather hadn't been sure of our father. He would never have said it was because he came from the East End, from a family of bookmakers and fishmongers, or that the car he drove was flash. Over the years Grandfather began to like him—he had started a business, bought a house, had a family, and continued to love his wife. Our father was one of the few people who could make Grandfather laugh.

"Well, I always said, Simon is a wide boy," Mrs. Stirling announced.

"What's a wide boy?" Eden asked.

"Never you mind," Grandfather said, giving Mrs. Stirling a disapproving look while she busied herself wiping the counter.

Mrs. Stirling had been at Caldhame close to twenty-five years. She had been with them when Anne left—in a taxi to the station to catch the London train. She helped cook their meals when they had no appetites, sitting at the table in the quiet house, hoping she would come back. She tried to interest our mother in needlepoint and the Bible. After so many years at Caldhame, Mrs. Stirling said whatever was on her mind.

As we sat at the table, I thought of the earring Mum had thrown in the gutter, the turquoise stones sinking to the bottom of the drain. Lost there, beneath the city streets, among the cigarette ends and sweets wrappers. Would they ever be a pair again? If one were to wash up on a riverbank, on a seashore, if someone, a woman, walking by the water, were to find one, to see one, she might not even bother to touch it, pick it up, rescue it from the other stones on the shore. By then, it would be dark with city grime and faded and worn from the salt and waves.

TWO

Eden and I walked up the narrow flight of stone steps to the round room at the top of the house. "How can someone build a perfect circle when it's so hard to draw one?" Eden said, as he looked around the room.

The ceiling was as high and pointed as a witch's hat. Sometimes birds and mice found their way inside and built their nests in the rafters, dropping leaves and twigs on the floor.

A hundred years ago or more, the house was an inn, a *cauld* house, on the drove road from the Highlands. A battle had been fought here: the battle of Sheriffmuir. Mrs. Stirling swears she's seen the ghosts of soldiers in the fields below.

Eden found a model airplane kit he had brought the last time we were here. He opened the box, but the pot of glue had dried.

I took a book from the bookshelf. It was called *The Perfect Daffodil* by Petra Patterson. I sat down in the green armchair, looking at the pictures. In the back of the book was a library card, and the last name written on the card was Anne Bruce, dated 12 June 1964.

Occasionally, our grandmother Anne came to visit us in London. She brought us presents from America: a set of towels from Bloomingdale's, a necklace for me, and a box of Legos for Eden. She looked young for her age, well dressed; on the street and in the shops and restaurants, people thought she was my mother. When they made this mistake, she would never correct them.

You could see in her now, like a picture in a frame, her regrets over leaving her daughter when she was a young girl. They had never been close and they never would be. My mother would say, not kindly, that Anne was trying to win us over with presents.

She came to London with her American husband, the accountant. They were staying at Claridges. The hotel room had a separate dressing room, with a single bed, which was made by the maids every morning with crisp white sheets, tucked tightly in the corners. She invited me to stay with them in the hotel for the weekend and I said yes.

My grandmother sipped her tea, she buttered a scone from a silver tray, with a stitched-up look on her mouth. She had never understood her daughter, especially her taste in men. When she first met my father, she took my mother away on holiday, in hopes that she would forget about him.

My mother said she had never been warm or affectionate. My mother said she had waited in bed at night with the light on, hoping she would come to kiss her good night, to tuck her in. She remembered sitting alone in the hallway, waiting for her to come home, but by then her mother was already in America.

My grandmother told me that, if I wanted to, I could come and spend the summer with her in America. They had a house by the beach. I nodded, I said I wanted to. That day, in the hotel with my grandmother, I was a different girl: the daughter she wanted me to be. Sharpening the blade of the knife, as I lay in the hotel sheets, I practiced the lines I would say to my mother when I told her I was leaving for the summer. Maybe I would say it was for longer—the school year, the rest of my life.

My grandmother bought two tickets to the ballet. First, she said, I needed a haircut and a new dress. We went to Harrods, to have my hair cut, like hers, in a straight line below the chin. Afterward, we walked down Hennington Square to the dress shop.

In the dress shop, there was a knitted striped shirt and skirt, hanging from the rack. The yarn had pieces of silver and gold thread in it, making it shine. But there was another girl looking through the clothes rack in the store, and she took the dress into the dressing room.

The girl was a year or two younger than I was. She had thick eyebrows and long dark hair, and now that she had the dress behind the curtain I wanted it even more. Her mother wore a veil and held an armful of dresses she was buying for her. The girl came from the dressing room and said she wanted the gold and silver dress too.

We chose another dress, navy velvet with black trim, to wear to the ballet. I watched as the mother in the veil laid dress after dress on the counter, buying them all for her daughter.

My grandmother and I walked through Kensington. I held the shopping bag with the dress wrapped in tissue paper inside; my hair, just washed and blown dry, fell softly around my face. I looked at my reflection in the shop windows as I held my grandmother's hand. Now we were going to have lunch at Saint Ambrosia.

"It's not fair that the other girl got the dress I wanted. She was pudgy." I said, my voice like a kite, because today I was someone else.

"They were rich Arabs," my grandmother said. "It's quite vulgar to buy a young girl so many expensive dresses."

We looked at the tea cakes and pastries, like jewels, behind the glass inside Saint Ambrosia.

At the ballet, we sat in a corner balcony. I held the binoculars to my eyes, but more than the dancers I wanted to look at the audience. I was trying to imagine the daily lives of the people here. The young brother and sister in matching sailor suits: I imagined the house those two children lived in and what they ate for breakfast. I stared at a large woman wrapped in fur, her fingers covered in rings.

Were her days like the day I had just spent with my grandmother, looking behind glass at pastries and dresses?

"This isn't working." Eden threw a piece of the model airplane against the floor. "The glue bottle's dried closed and all the paints have dried too."

"You don't have to have a tantrum."

He crossed his arms, staring at the wall.

Outside the day was darkening. The windows dropped pale squares of light around us.

"What do you think Dad's doing today?" Eden asked, looking up at me from where he sat on the floor.

"Oh, he's probably having a great time, lying on the sofa with his feet up, drinking a beer, smoking a joint, watching a Manchester game on the telly with no one at home to nag him."

I turned the pages of the book. I could feel Eden watching me and pretended to concentrate. A single fly buzzed in the room. He swatted at it, trying to distract himself from the thought of our father, happy without us.

"What are you reading about?" he said, looking over my shoulder.

"Oh, Eden. Can't I have one moment of peace?"

"I was just asking." Eden walked away from me, to the book-shelves. He touched the spines of the books. He went to the window, looking outside at the tree branches that touched the glass, where Red squirrels and birds would perch and peek inside, before flying away.

I used to believe that this was the tower where Robert the Bruce hid before the battle of Bannockburn. I pictured him lying on the floor in this room, staring up at the narrow windows. In this room, he would watch the small spider try to spin her web in a rounded corner. But the web wouldn't catch. She tried again and again until at last she succeeded and her web caught. That spider would inspire him to rise up for Scotland and fight the battle of Bannockburn.

I had told Eden this was the tower but never told him I was wrong. The tower Robert the Bruce hid in was miles from here.

Eden walked restlessly to a wooden door, shaped like an arch so it disappeared in the rounded walls. He turned the handle, but the door would not open. His face reddened as he pulled. "Why is this door locked?" He knelt down, peering through the keyhole. "All my games are in there."

I got up to have a look, but all I could see was the shape of the keyhole in a dark room. I remembered, then, that there was something inside I wanted too: a box of costume jewelry, which had belonged to my grandmother Anne. This year, at school, poppet beads had become fashionable again. Samantha Fenton wore them and Sheba Marks, whose mother was the fashion editor at *Harpers & Queen*. They sat in class at their desks, clicking and unclicking them from around their necks and wrists. I wanted to make that sound too.

Mrs. Stirling sat in a faded armchair reading a paperback in her lilac slippers with small purple bows. When she saw us, she covered the book with a tea towel, hiding the blond gladiator on the cover.

"Mrs. Stirling," Eden said, "the closet upstairs is locked and I can't open the door."

"Oh, you poor wee fellow," Mrs. Stirling said. "Why would it be locked? I'm not even sure if there's a key for it. It's probably just stuck."

"No," Eden said. "I can see that it's locked."

Mrs. Stirling groaned as she pushed herself up from her chair. She put her hand on the low of her back, as though these movements pained her. We followed her into the mudroom, where she pulled a footstool from beneath the coats.

"*Och*," she said. "Look up there, you'll see the key ring."

I stepped on the stool, holding the hat rack for balance.

All the keys were kept on one ring: the garden shed, the side door, the grandfather clock—keys that had lost their locks years ago but were never thrown away.

Eden carried the ring of keys upstairs. He tried them all, big and small, but none turned the lock. I was sitting in the armchair again, thinking about the string of poppets while I studied the pictures of sweets and puddings in a cookery book, when a thought occurred to me.

"Eden," I said. "You know, there's a window inside the cupboard."

"A small window," he said.

"Yeah, but you could fit through it."

"What do you mean?"

"Look, if you climb out onto the ledge and walk just a few feet to the window, all you have to do is open it and climb inside."

"Oh."

Eden looked out at the stone ledge, covered with damp leaves and bird droppings.

"I'll tie a rope around your waist. Let's go have a look in the toolshed."

In the damp toolshed, we found only rope so thick we could hardly bend it or string so thin it would only be good for tying to the end of a kite. Eden looked at the rusty tools, the bicycle with the missing wheel.

As we walked by the linen cupboard in the hall, Eden had an idea. "We could tie sheets together to make ropes," he said. It was a shame, I thought, as I took two clean white sheets from the shelves. They were crisp from the line.

We carried them up the stairs and tied them together.

Eden stood by the window as I tightened one end of the sheets around his waist and tied the other end to the water pole.

Eden stood on the radiator and pushed open the window. The damp air came in, like a breath.

"You have to walk with your back to the wall, Eden."

We had seen all the Pink Panther films.

He climbed out the window and onto the ledge, his hands still wrapped around the windowpane.

"May, Eden!" our mother called to us as she walked up the stairs. "Mrs. Stirling said you borrowed her keys, and she wants them back before she leaves today—"

She stopped in the doorway. She looked at the sheets tied to the water pole, stretching like a streamer across the room.

"Where's Eden?"

Then she saw him standing outside on the ledge, and ran to the window.

"Eden? What are you . . . ?" Her voice trailed behind her as she ran to the window. "Just stay still. Give me your hand."

She stood on her tiptoes, reaching up to him. Her hands clasped around his wrist and she pulled him in. Not gently, furiously. He fell forward into her arms, his knees hit the radiator below.

"Oh, God!" she yelled, when he was inside, as though relieved of a great weight.

"You hurt me," Eden said, rubbing his knees.

"What were you doing? Why were you on the window ledge?"

I sighed, rolling my eyes. "Because the cupboard door is stuck and he wanted to find his old toys. Jesus, Mum, calm down to a panic."

This enraged her more, and she turned to Eden. "You could have fallen! What if you fell? You'd be dead or in the hospital with broken bones, or worse things could have—"

"It's perfectly safe; the sheet is tied to the pipe."

She came toward me in a fury. Once, in the Fulham pool, when Eden didn't emerge quickly enough from his dive off the high board, she jumped in after him in all her clothes, shoes and winter coat, her handbag still in her hand flying up in the air.

"Untie that right now," she was saying to me. Before I could begin she was untying it herself, yanking at the knots. "Whose idea was this, May? You could have gotten him killed."

"It's only three flights up."

She stood flustered in the room, her hands out in the air. "Don't either of you have one drop of sense? Eden, the next time May wants you to do something stupid, tell me first. All right, darling?"

"He wanted his games," I said.

She took the key ring and told us to put the sheets back. "Supper's nearly ready," she said, as she left the room. We listened to her footsteps on the stairs, the jangle of keys in her hands.

The sheets lay on the floor, white and twisted, like a strangled ghost. A bird landed on the window ledge and then flew away. How would we get inside the cupboard now? I thought of the string of poppets, sitting in a wooden chest in the dark.

The sheets weren't folded as before; the crease of the new fold didn't match with the old. I put them back in the linen closet at the bottom of the pile, where Mrs. Stirling wouldn't see them until we were gone.

THREE

In the morning Mum, Eden, and I went for a walk across the moors. Eden swung his arms at his sides like a soldier. We walked into a soft breeze that blew our hair back. The dogs ran ahead and up the hill where the sheep grazed. Eden held a handful of grass out to the sheep, but they backed away.

"They don't like you," I said, as I marched past him up to the top of the hill.

From the hilltop we could see the countryside below: the fields and the farms and the houses in between. It was springtime, and all around the flowers were in bloom. The dogs rolled on their backs, kicking their legs in the air. "Look," Eden said, pointing to them. "They're only as tall as the dandelions."

Eden blew a dandelion into the wind. Our mother stood with her hands in her coat pockets, looking out at the different shades of green fields below.

"Mum?" Eden said.

"Yes, darling?"

"Are we going back to London soon?"

She turned, looking at him. "We're having a nice walk in the country, aren't we?"

Eden looked away; a sudden flush of shame. "I was just wondering."

Below, the dark and pale green fields, the train and the track, the church and the steeple, looked simple. Cars moved slowly along the roads, safe as toys. The pale blue sky and the clouds, so certain above us; it seemed that nothing so small as a lost earring or the wrong question asked would cause any harm.

On our way back to Grandfather's, we stopped at the dairy for a pail of milk. Margaret, the farmer's wife, stood outside the barn. She wore a striped knit sweater, jeans, and green Wellingtons that came to her knees. Her wavy red hair was tied in a bun at the base of her neck. She rested one arm on the stone wall, standing at a slant, like a man.

"Did you hear about Kirsty O'Conner?" Margaret was saying to Mum. "She lives in Paris now, left her husband."

"Did she?"

"She met this man, you see. . . ."

Eden hit the wall with a stick he'd found on the ground. I sat on the wall while Margaret and Mum gossiped about their old schoolmates. The dogs lay in a shallow puddle to cool their bellies.

"What about Ian Brodie?" I heard my mother ask. She had dated him in school but complained that he had never tried to even kiss her.

Their voices were a seesaw.

"He turned the family butcher into a fruit and flower shop. His father must be turning, but everyone knew he was a queer one from the start. . . ."

Outside the barn, I saw a boy standing by the gate. He looked about my age, fourteen or fifteen. He had dark brown hair and skin the same cream color as his sweater. He held on to the railing as he stared out at the field.

"Nicholas!" Margaret called, and the boy turned, startled by the sound of her voice. "Fetch a pale of milk for the visitors. And mind it doesn't spill over the sides this time."

Margaret turned to my mother. In a whisper she said, "Now I'm stuck looking after the boy too. He's Donald's nephew, you see, and he came to live with us after his mother died."

After his mother died, she said, like a passing car.

"Why did she die?" Mum asked.

"Cancer."

"Where's his father?"

"Still in the pub, I suppose."

"That's terrible."

"It is," Margaret said, pushing up her sweater sleeves. "He's from the city. We hope we can make him useful around here."

This is the wind and this is the rocks. Margaret takes the calves from their mothers. It's business. A cow, a boy, a father in the pub. Whoever you are in the world, pain is pain.

Nicholas returned from the barn, carrying a pail of milk. "Is the milk still warm?" Margaret asked him.

"Yes," he said, glancing up at us. When I saw his eyes, it was like a surprise—a flash of a blue wing, a sparkling stone. I was thinking, as he walked closer: This boy, with the milk pail at his side— his mother just died.

FOUR

I made a bread pudding with stale raisin buns, while Mrs. Stirling told me the details of her youngest daughter Julie's upcoming wedding day. There would be a three-tiered sponge cake with white and pink columns and her seven nieces for flower girls. And the dress! An exact replica of the one Princess Diana wore.

The rain fell against the windowpanes; in the distance, I thought I saw a woman standing alone in the field.

The woman was my mother. The rain fell harder.

"What are you looking at out there?" Mrs. Stirling asked.

I turned away from the window. "Where's the cinnamon?"

"Who's that standing out in the pouring rain? Is that Lucy?" Mrs. Stirling said, wiping the condensation from the window with a tea towel. Then she watched from the window, standing with her hands on her hips. "Good lord, whatever is she doing? I tell you, she'll catch her death one of these days. You would never find me going for a walk without the proper clothes and let myself get caught in the pouring rain. But you see, I'm much more practical, and my Julie—she's the most sensible of all."

Mrs. Stirling: as practical as the pots and pans.

"It's in your blood, on the women's side. Your grandmother was the same: away with the pixies."

I touched the ends of my plaits. My mother walked slowly through the field, looking down, as though she had lost something in the long grass.

"She's only taking a walk and got caught in the rain."

"What's that?" Mrs. Stirling asked.

I shook my head.

"You're an awful mumbler."

"I said, she's only taking a walk."

Mrs. Stirling made a *tut-tut* sound with her mouth. "Temper, temper."

As Mum neared the house, I saw that her hair was dark and wet from the rain and her sweater hung heavy, close to her body. Soon she would be at the front door. Soon she would be home, the damp wind rushing in behind her. She'd be cold, shivering, in her wet clothes. Her face flushed and awake, she'd put her cool hands on my cheeks and kiss me hello.

It rained the rest of the weekend. Our mother spent the days in front of the fire with a blanket on her lap, reading old copies of *Country Life*. Eden asked Grandfather to tell him stories of the war. Mostly, he wanted to know about airplanes, tanks, and guns. Mosquitoes and Spitfires. Grandfather described the fighter planes, but he never talked about himself or the people he knew who had died.

When the rain stopped, I brushed my hair in front of the mirror, made sure my face was clean, and put on shiny lip gloss. Eden and I were taking the dogs for a walk, past the dairy farm. We walked down the dirt road, and soon we could smell the cows. It was milking time; the farmer led them down the lane.

We walked past the farmer's house. I leaned against the stone wall, pretending to tie my shoe. The windows of the house stared down like a guard dog. I looked into the field, but I did not see the boy.

*   *   *

Outside of Grandfather's, Eden threw a tennis ball for the dogs. The sky was as white as the house. In the distance, we could hear the sound of a car coming up the drive.

A small red car appeared around the bend. It was our father's car, a red Porsche meant to be driven fast, but he drove it slowly, for fear of scratching the bottom or splashing mud up the sides. He only drove the car for show. Every other week, he washed the car with a bucket of soapy water on the street.

The things he owned, he kept well. His father was a book-maker: things came and went, were won and lost in bets: a grand-father clock, a gold watch. . . .

The car pulled up to the house. He opened the car door and the dogs ran to him. They leapt and jumped, pawing his trousers with their claws.

"Shoo, shoo, you horrible creatures!" he said, stepping away from them. When he said the word *horrible,* it sounded like *orrible.*

Eden let the tennis ball fall from his hands. He ran across the grass and over the gravel to him.

"Is that my favorite boy?" Dad said, holding his arms open wide. Eden ran to him, crashing against him like a wave. His face pressed against his father's chest, he closed his eyes for a moment, as though he would sleep there.

I stood outside the doorway, watching them.

"Hello, sweetness, aren't you going to say hello to your father?"

The wind felt cool through the knit in my cardigan. Mum came from the house. She stood in the doorway with her arms crossed in front of her and a sour look on her face. From the wind or him?

"Well, you're a cheerful bunch," he said. "Glad I came for a visit. At least there's one good-natured person in the family." He put his arm around Eden and Eden beamed. Another kiss, another squeeze, and he'd take off like a rocket ship.

Dad ran his fingers through his hair, glancing at his reflection in the window of the car. He was dressed in a fitted brown corduroy suit, with a scarf tied around his neck and handmade brown boots.

"I've come to apologize. Even though, quite frankly, darling, I have no fucking idea what I'm apologizing for."

Mum looked away, as though studying the hinge on the door.

"Oh, come on, Lucy, don't be stupid. I've driven all the way up from London. Had to leave Sebastian in charge of the shop, and you know I hate to do that. You could at least give me a kiss hello."

Mum let her arms drop to her sides.

He walked toward her. "Let's kiss and make up, what do you say, Lucy?"

Her eyes went low and soft when she looked at him, his lips close to hers. It seemed, in the moment before they kissed, that her lips turned from pink to red. They swelled, they puckered, they parted like flowers before his lips touched hers.

The wind blew; the leaves rattled. The dogs lay still on the ground. The sky behind them went light to dark blue. He held his arm around her waist. They kissed slowly, parting for breath, and kissed again.

We had tea by the fire. Eden bunched up pieces of an old newspaper, while Grandfather piled the kindling. He let Eden light the long match and touch the flame to the paper, which sent a sudden blaze of red into the room.

A tray of tea sat on the table; milk, sugar, and a plate of biscuits the dogs stared at, waiting to take one from the plate and swallow it whole.

My father read the *Dunblane Daily* police report aloud in his actorly Scottish accent.

The reported incidence of women's knickers stolen from the clothesline has risen to twenty-five. We are advising women not to leave their undergarments unattended on the washing line.

Mum sat next to him, giggling like a schoolgirl. I stared ahead at the flames of the fire.

"Oh, Mrs. Stirling," Dad said, when she walked in the room. "Haven't you heard? Don't leave your knickers on the clothesline, no more. They might get pinched by the knicker thief."

Mrs. Stirling gave him a disapproving look. "Don't worry your pretty little head about it, Simon. I hang my smalls over the stove to dry," she said as she left the room.

"Mind you, the knicker thief would probably mistake hers for pillowcases," he whispered to Eden. Eden's face was red from the fire, and now he couldn't stop laughing. Jokes about knickers and bums were the funniest things.

Our father smiled at our mother as he lifted the teacup to his lips. His eyes went straight to hers—a sparkle, a light, a reflection of the flame in his dark eyes. She leaned her head against his shoulder.

"I was wondering how long it would take you to come and try to woo me back," she said softly.

"Have I succeeded yet?"

"I think so."

He had brought Grandfather a bottle of scotch and a box of glazed dates, wrapped in a box with a thin silver fork. I wondered if he would open them tonight, after supper, and if we would stay up late with the fire.

One night, the last time we were here, Dad put a record on and did imitations of Mum and her friends dancing at Annabel's. We had laughed so hard, Grandfather too, that our eyes watered. Even Mum, who sometimes cried when he made fun of her.

You could never tell with Mum until it was too late. Sometimes she would laugh at first; then her face would break, like a plate, and she would burst into tears. But that night, when he put the record on and danced, we all laughed.

FIVE

We drove back to London Sunday afternoon.

Eden and I had several days' worth of lessons to make up. Mrs. Jenkins gave me a warning. "If you miss any more school, I will have to hold you back. You don't want to be the tallest and the oldest in your form, do you?"

We stood outside the classroom door. She wore a necklace made of seashells that fell against her collar bone.

"No. I don't, Mrs. Jenkins," I said, holding the sides of my uniform skirt. "But my mum was the one who took us away."

"Well, I will have to speak to your mother about this."

"Yes, you should," I said. "She should be told off, Mrs. Jenkins."

"That's quite enough, young lady."

In the shop, SIMON'S, Mum said she was a glorified salesgirl. When they were deciding on a name for the shop, my father thought that his would be the best. SIMON'S was painted in deep green on the windows. "Quite catchy, don't you think?" He stood with his hands in his pockets, admiring his name on the storefront windows.

After work, they came home and cooked supper together. She helped me with my French, which she spoke well, because when she was sixteen she ran away from boarding school, where they only let her wash her hair with dry shampoo, and went to live with her

French boyfriend. She helped Eden with his reading, pointing to each word on the page.

Our father was a good cook but useless with homework. He dropped out of school when he was thirteen and went to work with his cousins in the East End selling things that "fell off the back of a lorry."

"There has to be more for us," our mother said, as she washed the dishes in the sink, "than working in the shop all day. Don't you think? . . . Simon?"

He stared at the television; *East Enders* was on. A half-smoked joint lay in the ashtray, a box of Rose's chocolates on his lap that he picked the toffees out of, saving them for himself. The bright cellophane wrappers sprinkled the table like confetti.

"What's that, Lucy?" he asked, during the advert.

"Nothing, Simon," she said. He had answered too late.

Eden dried the dishes with a dish towel. I wiped the table clean, sweeping the crumbs onto the floor.

Our father stared at the television. "Good advert, this one is. I heard they spent close to a million pounds on it. Blimey."

Our mother left the dishes in the sink. She turned to him as though she would say something else but only let out a breath. She walked to the garden doors and pushed them open, too impatient to undo them. The latch fell from the frame to the floor as she opened the doors, letting the evening air come through.

"Lucy?" our father said, standing up angrily. "What are you doing? You just broke the latch!" He picked it up from the floor, the bronze hook, holding it in the palm of his hand. She had walked outside to the end of the garden, where she stood in front of the brick wall.

SIX

In June, school let out for the summer holidays. It was a cool summer in London and rained most afternoons. Eden and I wandered through the city, spending hours at the Fulham pool, swimming until our lips and fingers pruned, then buying salt and vinegar crisps from the machines. We walked home with wet hair and the taste of the pool water and the crisps mixing in our mouths.

On weekend nights, Mum and Dad invited their friends around for a barbecue in the garden: Annabel; Suzy and her boyfriend Jim; Rochelle, the fashion designer, her husband, Steven, and their three children. They sat around the table rolling joints and drinking wine while the meat on the grill smoked behind them, talking about how they were going to improve the world with their shops and magazines.

I mistook a square cut of hash for a piece of chocolate and spat it half chewed into my hand. The speakers faced out of the windows so the music played in the garden and I couldn't wash the taste from my mouth. Upstairs, the three other children, Eden, and I dressed in our fancy dress costumes and rehearsed a play for the grown-ups. As the summer evening grew dark, we dared each other to eat flower petals, thinking they would either be poisonous or make us high, and then fell asleep on the living room floor in front of the television.

* * *

One evening, our father came home from work with a bouquet of tall pale, yellow flowers wrapped in tissue paper, and a bottle of wine for our mother.

"These are for you, my darling," he said, kissing her on the lips by the kitchen sink.

She held the flowers in her arms, their stems tied with a bow of twine.

"These are beautiful," she said, as he wrapped her in his arms.

I was standing at the sink washing the green beans, and Eden was sitting at the table with his coloring pencils, tracing airplanes.

"You'll never guess who phoned today."

"Who?"

He kissed the back of her neck, then let her go.

"Remember Mitch Carson, the producer, who moved to India?"

"Oh, right. Yeah," she said.

"Anyway, he phones me at the shop. I haven't spoken to him in ages, mind you. He tells me he's selling all his earthly possessions to follow the Maharaji and would I like them for the shop? Well, yes, thank you, I said, and booked myself on a flight to Delhi next week."

"What? You're joking."

He shook his head. "He's got some fabulous antiques. Don't you remember his house on Munster Road? He had that beautiful armoire."

"Vaguely," she said, her voice sounding lost.

"Dad," Eden said, "*Top of the Pops* is on tonight!" A loud happy-sounding sentence, floating like a balloon through the kitchen.

"Maybe I'll pick up some new dance moves to do at the clubs," he said jokingly to Eden, but really he was watching her. "Lucy," he said, the tone of his voice settling. "Lucy what's the matter?"

"How long will you be gone?" she asked him.

"It's just for a couple of weeks, until I can ship all the stuff back. Mind you, with the Indian post you never know how long that will be."

Sometimes, when Dad talked about India or was talking to Raj, the Indian man who owned the corner shop, he put on a comical Indian accent. "Two hundred rupees, it's cheap! I swear, if you don't believe me, ask my brother!"

I would look away, embarrassed and worried that Raj would be upset by this, but Raj always laughed, touching him affectionately on the shoulder and giving Eden and me a rose-flavored sweet wrapped in wax paper that he took from a box behind the counter.

She looked at the flowers lying nearby. "Why don't we all go?" she said. "It's school summer holidays, and I've always wanted to go back to India."

When they had first met, my mother had been attracted to Dad because he was interested in spirituality. They traveled to India together to meet the Maharaji. When I was younger, I would find them in their bedroom, meditating in front of the mirror or upside down in shoulder stand. India was where Dad had had the idea to import furniture for his shop in London.

"All of us?" he said now, looking from Eden to me. Looking as though she had just asked him to lift the house off the ground. "Lucy, I'm just making a quick trip to do a bit of business. Let's not make a big thing of it. Besides, who would mind the shop while we were gone?"

Mum let out a breath. "How about Sebastian? He can look after things while we're away. Is our whole life going to revolve around the shop?"

The green beans sat in a bowl of cool water. She insulted the shop; they'll fight all night.

A shadow crossed my father's face. "Excuse me, Lucy," he said angrily. "I'm about to get on a seventeen-hour flight to India in the middle of monsoon season. I care about the shop. How do you think we bought the house? How do you think we pay the bills? Who pays for May's ballet lessons?"

"I don't take ballet, Dad."

Dad looked at me, confused. He gestured to the wine on the counter. "These things cost money. I work hard."

"Well, I work hard too, but unlike you I don't find it as satisfying. Selling overpriced, useless things to rich people."

"Well, wouldn't it be nice to not care about money like you."

They stood facing each other. The silence fell between them like shards of glass. The bottle of wine sat on the counter. Eden held the pencil tightly in his hand.

My mother stepped back. "May, will you set the table?"

I opened the drawer, counting: four knives, four forks.

Dad lifted the flowers from the counter; the wrapping made a rustling sound. He opened the cupboard and carefully, with both hands, took down a tall glass vase, the opening shaped like a flower. He rinsed the vase at the sink and filled it with cold water.

"Nice flowers, don't you think?" he said, glancing at her. "I bought them from the Covent Garden florist; they were one pound fifty a stem."

He loved to tell the price of things. His favorite story was the antique Indian crib he found outside an orphanage and paid twenty rupees for. He shipped it back to London and sold it in his shop for three hundred pounds, to a woman who wanted it for her flower pots.

Mum floured the pieces of flounder and laid them on a plate. She stepped back from the stove when the oil sizzled. Was the argument over? I had a nervous feeling. There was a line in the palm of my hand where I'd held the knives and forks.

I walked around the table, from chair to chair, laying down napkin, fork, knife.

Mum took the potatoes from the oven with a mitt, dropping them on the wooden counter. Did she feel satisfied now, cutting open the baked potatoes?

Our father arranged the flowers in the vase, stepping back to view them.

"Dad, will you be back in time for my birthday?"

I put a knife and fork on either side of Eden's coloring book. "That's not till August, Eden," I said softly, as I laid the napkin down. "He's just going for a couple of weeks. You only think about yourself."

Eden looked up at me, as though I had pinched him.

Mum carried the plates to the table. "They're pretty," she said, glancing at the flowers.

Our father looked at the flowers, their yellow petals reflected on his skin. Did he feel satisfied? Full of himself, the thrill of his own business, counting the money at the end of the day. A working-class boy, he had pulled himself up in the world.

"To us!" he would say with his friends in the pub. If only his father could see him now; turning the key to lock up his shop. On his way home, picking up a bottle of wine from the wine merchant, walking up the street to the house he almost owned. A house in a good location. A house with the lights on.

The little things: turning the windup watch his father had won in a race, a good cup of tea like his mother made, watching the *East Enders* at the end of the day. Money in the bank. These things would fill him up.

We sat down at the table. The fish and potatoes steamed on the plates. "Delicious fish," he said.

"It's from Mullon's," she said, as she forked the lemon.

What if then he had said, Why don't you come with me, Lucy? That's not a bad idea, after all. What if then he had gone to her and put his arms around her, saying, We'll go together, have a summer holiday.

He looked at her, checking her face, which had no expression at all, to see if it had changed. The four of us, in a row of airplane seats to India. Like leaves on a stem; our lives pointing in a new direction.

He spread the napkin across his lap. That might be quite nice actually. Even if he had wanted to, his next thought would have been, But then, who will watch the shop? It would have to be Sebastian. The last time he had left an employee for longer than a few days, the shop had been burgled and money had been lost.

SEVEN

Our mother managed the shop while our father was away in India. Sebastian helped out part-time during the week. He played the piano and was the lead singer in a band called Diamond Eyes. Sometimes, he played tape cassettes of his band on the shop stereo and set the fliers for his shows on the counter. He sat on the tall stool, behind the counter, in a thin plaid shirt, suede trousers, and boots, writing lyrics in his journal.

> *I went to a party*
> *With my friend named Marty.*
> *We kissed by the kitchen sink,*
> *she was pretty, I think.*

Sebastian liked working in the shop. Keith Richards stopped by occasionally, and so did Annie Lennox. Because of the famous clientele, Sebastian admired Simon, and because Simon knew he was admired, he liked Sebastian.

Mum paid me five pounds a day to babysit Eden while she worked in the shop and on the weekend mornings so she could have a rest.

For breakfast, I made Weetabix with warm milk and honey, and we let Porridge lick the cream from the foil milk cap. After breakfast we collected any money we could find lying around the house—in coat pockets, under sofa cushions—and sometimes we would sneak into the bedroom while our mother slept quietly taking the change from the dresser, careful not to wake her.

The last time Eden woke her, touching her shoulder and whispering in her ear, "It's time to wake up, Mum. It's morning." She rolled away from him as though he had frightened her. "Why did you do that?" she said, waking angrily. "I was having the most amazing dream. Now I'll never know what happens in the end."

At the sweet shop, we considered each jar carefully, debating the cost and what would be the best mixture. The customers came and went.

"Are you planning on spending the night?" the shopkeeper asked us. When we left, the weather had changed. The day had brightened and the blue sky appeared behind broken clouds.

We walked down the road to the toy shop, Tiger, Tiger. "May, what would you choose?" Eden asked, stopping in front. "If you could have anything you wanted?"

I looked in the windows at the train tracks running through a miniature town, at a box of magic tricks. I was too old for these things now. I stared at my reflection in the glass. I was wearing my denim miniskirt and a white T-shirt with blue dots on it. I tilted my head to the side. I was fourteen but thought I could pass for fifteen.

We walked past an old woman sitting on the bench with her granddaughter. The old woman held a napkin in her hand, smiling as she watched her.

We had always spent the summer days with our other grandmother, our father's mother Nanny Hannah, but she died this past winter. Sometimes still, when I woke up, I would think, Let's visit Nanny

Hannah today. We'll take the bus, she'll cook us lunch and take a Victoria sponge cake she bought at Marks & Spencer from the freezer, and Eden and I will help her hang the washing on the line. I had these thoughts before remembering that she was dead.

On Sundays, Mum, Dad, Eden, and I would go round to Nanny Hannah's. She lived in a ground-floor flat in Maida Vale. Our father helped her with the bills, after her husband Jacko died five years ago, from drinking too much after a horse race. They found him ice cold on the pavement.

"Hello, my loves," Hannah would say when she greeted us at the door. My father would hand her flowers and a box of chocolates we had bought for her on the way. She always dressed for our visit, set her hair, put on a bit of lipstick. She was a heavyset woman with a gravelly voice from smoking.

"Flattering ensemble, Mum," our father would say.

"You like it?" she would ask, turning slightly to the side in her tartan two-piece. "I bought it on sale at Marks the other day." She would say this as though the shop were an old friend. When she bent to pick something off the floor, she would put her hand on her lower back and say, "Oh, me aching back." People said she looked like the Queen Mum but with a Cockney accent, a compliment that made her blush and set her hair the same way and dress in two-piece suits and matching hats.

In the flat, my father would settle into the comfortable chair by the flame heater and read the paper or watch a game on the telly while Hannah cooked lunch. She was a delicious cook; everything she made was tasty. On Sundays she made us a roast chicken with rosemary potatoes and bread sauce. In the summer she made salmon cakes and egg salad. She sliced whole potatoes into thick chips and fried them in a frying pan of oil until they were golden brown. She grilled haddock and cod and served it with tartar sauce and horseradish. She made trifle in a glass bowl so you could see the layers of

custard, jam, and sponge cake. My mother said the reason her cooking was so good was because she cooked with love.

"Mum," my father would say, raising his teacup, "you make
the best cup of tea in England."

We ate at the small table in the room with the heater. Our
parents never fought at Hannah's, and Eden and I spent the
day looking at her things. A cut-glass bowl of sweets sat on the
sitting room table on a lace cloth; we wondered how she could
have bowls of sweets around and not eat them all in one day. Her
sewing kit opened like a fan into different layers and compart-
ments. She took Eden and me round the corner to her friend's
flat, to show us off. She took us to the park across the street and
sat on the bench for hours while we played. I always felt, with her,
a little younger than I was: watched over and cared for. After she
died, I prayed to her.

As she grew older, there was a flattened look in her eyes, a faraway fear; you could see it when we said good-bye on Sunday eve-
nings. We would put on our coats in the hall, dimly lit by a chandelier.

"I'll see you next week," she would say. "Give me a ring, let
me know what you fancy, so I can make it to the shops in time."
Our father would slip a twenty-pound note into her hand.

As Hannah stood in the doorway, she held her cardigan closed
with her hand, her toweling slippers on and a packet of cigarettes
and a gold-plated lighter in her pocket. She would wave, watching
us as we walked down the street.

The spring before she died, Eden and I spent a week at her
house during the Easter holidays. When she moved from the East
End to Maida Vale, Maida Vale had not been considered a desir-
able neighborhood. But London was changing; prices had risen and
younger, more fashionable people were moving in.

It was a warm day, and in Hannah's kitchen we packed a picnic to take to the park. Hannah made us egg sandwiches with
chopped onion on Portuguese buns, wrapped in wax paper. She

packed a cold bottle of fizzy lemonade, three paper cups, and a packet of chocolate biscuits. Even though we were only going to the small park down the road, she had dressed up a bit: powdered her face, put on lipstick, pinned her hair back.

As we were leaving, Hannah realized she had forgotten her reading glasses and went back in to get them. Eden and I sat on the wall outside, waiting for her. The daffodils planted in the park had grown tall but had not yet opened.

We waited on the warm limestone wall while two men in their late twenties, dressed in dark suits, talked outside the building. From the brochures in their hands, I could see they were the estate agents. The taller man pointed to the ground-floor flat with the wrong end of his pen.

"This one, the ground floor, has two bedrooms. It's being let for next to nothing now, to an old lady. But I don't expect she'll be around for much longer: fingers crossed," he said to the other one, who laughed uncomfortably.

The men had not seen Hannah open her front door. She stood on the doorstep with her key in her hand. By the expression on her face, I knew she had heard what the estate agent had said and had also heard the other man laugh in response. She fumbled, putting the key inside her purse, and looked unsure of how to step from the doorway to the pavement.

The estate agents walked on to the next row of flats without seeing her. Hannah walked slowly from the doorway. She stopped to look at the daffodils in the boxes. In the crook of her arm, she held a dark green carry bag from Harrods, with a section of the paper folded, to read in the park.

"Nice day, isn't it?" she said, looking down the street at the two men.

In the park, she sat down on the bench while Eden raced to the swing set. I laid out the picnic blanket on the grass but realized she would sit on the bench. I unpacked the sandwiches she had made, but when I offered her one she shook her head. The crossword section of the newspaper lay on the bench beside her.

She sat on the bench in the park, looking at the children in the playground, and then closed her eyes for a moment, tilting her face toward the sky to catch the last of the afternoon sun.

Eden and I walked to the river to look at the houseboats. Slowly, the boats and barges passed by. We spent a long time, deciding which houseboat we would want to live in, if we could.

The smell of brine from the river mixed in with the city air. Two men fished on the banks below the river wall, wearing caps with brims and rubber boots to their knees. Eden leaned forward over the wall, looking down at the water.

"Remember the time Dad said he was cooking Porridge for breakfast?"

"Yeah."

"That was funny, wasn't it?" His voice sounded uncertain, as though he was trying to rearrange the memory of it.

The morning Eden was talking about, we had come down to breakfast and seen Dad stirring a bubbling pot of porridge. "Morning, dustbin lids."

"What are you cooking?" Eden asked, excitedly.

"Porridge," Dad said, winking at me.

The pot was pale gray, the color of our cat. "Almost ready," he said, tasting it from the wooden spoon. "Just mind the toenails."

Eden's lips quivered; he still looked like a baby when he cried. After a moment of silence, he began to sob. He cried so hard, he hardly made a sound.

"Oh, we're only joking, you silly boy," Dad said, trying to comfort him.

Mum came into the kitchen, her hair in a towel, wet from the bath. "What's the matter, Eden?" she asked, but he could not answer her. "Why is he crying?" She looked at me and Dad.

"He thinks Dad's cooking the cat."

She knelt down by Eden, and he buried his face between her neck and shoulders. "You've really upset him."

"We were just having a laugh," he said. "I didn't know he was going to get so upset."

She looked up at Dad. "Why would you tell him that? You just don't think, do you?"

The table was set: a bowl of brown sugar, a bowl of strawberries, cream, and sliced pears. A tulip in a glass and a present in a small box wrapped in gold tissue paper. It was our mother's birthday.

We crossed the bridge to the park. The sky was clear—no rain today—and we sat down on the bench.

"May," Eden said, "if you were stranded on an island and you could only have one type of sweet, what would you choose?"

I shook my head. "I don't know. What would you choose?"

Eden stared down at the rubber ground beneath the swings. "I'm not absolutely sure, but probably Smarties."

"That's a terrible choice. They'd all melt together in the sun and turn an ugly greenish color, like they did when we left them in the glove compartment."

"Oh, yeah." Eden hit the palm of his hand against his forehead. "I forgot about that."

The pigeons reflected in the rain puddles as they flew up and away from us. I thought they were pretty, the gray and white pigeons. A woman sitting on a bench pushed a pram back and forth with her foot while she read a magazine. After a while, she closed her magazine and stood up, straightened the back of her skirt, and wheeled the pram out of the playground.

Soon another woman took her place on the bench, a young mother with short brown hair wearing long beaded earrings. She crossed one leg on top of the other, blowing cigarette smoke over her shoulder, while her two boys shouted and chased each other around the swing and the slide.

EIGHT

"Oh, lovely. That sounds lovely," I heard Greta say, as I walked into our house. "Is it near the beach?"

Greta was Eden's babysitter when I wasn't available. She was twenty and wanted to be a television actress. She was pretty—"In a very English-looking way," Annabel would say. Annabel was my mother's friend, who decided who was pretty and who had style, in real life and in films and magazines.

"Is what near the beach?" I asked, from the doorway.

Mum looked at me as she clasped an earring to her ear. "I thought you were spending the night at Julia's house."

"She has the chicken pox."

"Didn't she have them as a child? Well, Greta's already canceled her plans for the evening."

"I don't mind," Greta said. "I'll stay here with May. We can read the latest *Hello!*" A red suede purse with her name, Greta, written in rhinestones, hung off the back of the kitchen chair.

"We have the new *Vogue* too."

Eden came from the garden with two wet action figures in his hands, that he had left overnight in the terrapin pond to see if they would sink. He sat down beside Greta and sipped a glass of Ribena.

"The fish fingers are in the fridge and the carrots are in the pot on the stove," Mum told Greta.

Mum wore her tight jeans, with high-heeled cork sandals and a short-sleeved brown silk shirt.

Greta put her hand on Eden's back. "You like fish fingers, don't you?"

"I shouldn't be back too late," Mum said.

She kissed all of us, Eden, Greta, and me, leaving a wine-colored mark on our cheeks. She stopped in front of the mirror in the hall, picking up her keys and purse, looking at her reflection from the side.

"You look quite sexy," Greta said, with a wink.

After supper, Greta went upstairs to make sure Eden had taken his bath. I turned on the telly, but it was all news. The royal family was leaving for their summer holiday at Balmoral. Princess Diana was in Cambodia trying to rid the country of land mines. Margaret Thatcher was discussing the recent row in the House of Lords. I sat on the sofa and counted the mirrored pieces in the Indian pillow, waiting for Greta. Last week, she had told me stories about her boyfriend, Trevor, and I was hoping she would tell me more tonight.

When I grew bored with waiting, I went upstairs to look for her. She was in my mother's room, looking at the clothes in her wardrobe. "It's chilly in this house," she said, when she saw me. "I was just looking for a sweatshirt or something warm to put on."

"Her sweaters are in the drawer. Have you had any more dates with Trevor?"

Greta picked up a perfume bottle from the dresser and dotted it on her wrists. Humming a song to herself, she lifted the lid from an apple carved out of wood and peeked inside.

"That's Mum's button collection," I told her.

"Fascinating," Greta said, letting the lid drop. "Look, I just have to use the loo and then I'll come downstairs."

In the kitchen, I took the biscuit tin down from the top of the cupboard. Last week, Greta told me a sexy story about Trevor and

I had it memorized. It went like this: "First Trevor kissed me. He kissed me for such a long time. He is absolutely the best kisser!" She said *kisser* like *kissa*.

We had been sitting on the sofa in the living room. I hugged a pillow to my chest, listening to the story. "So then he put his thigh between my legs and rubbed it up and down; that's what boys do to make you feel really sexy. Then he pulled my knickers down and put his fingers in my pussy."

"Oh!" I said, and felt a pinch right between my legs.

"He called me juicy. That's what he said he likes, juicy girls."

All week I'd been waiting to find out what happened next. Sometimes, I thought about it happening to me, but not with Trevor, with a different boy: Nicholas, the boy I had seen at the dairy in Scotland. I licked the chocolate from the top of the digestive biscuit and looked down the hallway.

"You have chocolate all over your face," Greta said, when she walked into the kitchen. She took her packet of cigarettes from the table and lit one with her pink lighter.

"Did you see Trevor this week?"

Greta closed her eyes as she blew the smoke from her mouth. She shook her head no. "He hasn't phoned."

"Are you going to phone him?"

"I won't phone him again. That's not what ladies are supposed to do." She walked to the sink and dropped her ashes in it. "You know, the other week, when we went to the films?"

I nodded.

"I was so embarrassed to be seen with you."

I looked at Greta. I thought she was going to make a joke.

"Your coat had stains all down the front and your hair was greasy. Don't you ever wash it? I remember when you were younger and I used to pick you up from school, you were the most raggedy-looking girl in the playground. And your mum's so pretty and dresses so nicely and so does your father." She put out her cigarette in the sink. "I want you to get your shoes and practice putting them on."

"I know how to put them on."

She put one hand on her hip. "If you ever want me to take you to the films again or go anywhere with you, you'll get them."

I stood up from the table and walked down the hall to the front door where we left our shoes. Earlier that day I had done the vacuuming and I brought all our shoes that had gathered by the door upstairs. The only ones left were my Wellingtons, lying on their side and still damp inside from the rain.

One night, Greta had brought over her beauty kit and laid out all her makeup on a towel on my bedroom floor. She taught me how to apply rouge to accent my cheekbones, eyeliner for bigger, brighter eyes, and the lip liner for full pouty lips. This is what Greta does: she helps me look my best.

I brought my boots into the kitchen.

"Practice putting them on and taking them off fifteen times," Greta said. She pulled a chair away from the table and sat in front of me. I sat down on the kitchen step, but Greta shook her head. "You have to do it standing up."

If my mother had told me to do this, I never would have. I saw my reflection in the garden window, standing on the step under the hanging light, but I was just moving. Pulling one boot on, then the other, waiting for Greta to approve. The boots rubbed against the blister on my heel as I pulled them on and off.

Afterward, Greta filled the kitchen sink with hot water and fairy liquid. "Okay, now we're going to practice washing your face, but put your boots away first." In the sink were dishes, her cigarette ashes, and the kitchen sponge.

I carried my boots to the mat by the front and stood them up neatly, next to each other. I walked slowly. The hallway was dark and the only light came through the pane of glass above the front door.

When I was younger, some days Greta would pick me up from school and take me home. One day, on our way home, I asked if we could stop somewhere so I could use the toilet.

"Why didn't you use the loo at school?" she said. "Now you'll have to wait until we get home. The public toilets are dirty."

Greta said it was such a beautiful day she wanted to walk the long way around the common. The weather was warm and an ice cream lorry stopped across the street. "Should we stop and get one?" Greta said. I wanted one but I shook my head, in a hurry to get home. "Oh, but I'd really fancy one." She walked toward the lorry. She told me she would buy me one, but I was too uncomfortable to eat. We were almost home when Greta saw a pair of shoes she liked in a shop window and went inside to try them on.

On the doorstep of our house, she rummaged through her bag looking for the key: purse, coat pockets, jeans pockets. I stood with my legs crossed on the doorstep. When she unlocked the door, I ran inside and started up the stairs to the toilet, but Greta grabbed the straps of my overalls.

"You have to take your shoes off first."

"What?"

"It's a rule your mother made. They make the carpet dirty."

I was wearing lace-up boots, double-knotted. I felt an ache below my stomach, a pain, and a swell. I couldn't hold it anymore and wet myself on the floor by the front door.

"You're too old to wet yourself," Greta said, looking at the wet mark on the floor, the dark patch of denim down my legs.

As punishment for wetting the floor, she said, I had to wear my wet overalls for the rest of the day and was not allowed to change.

I walked up the stairs to my room. I was alone in the bedroom but afraid to change my clothes. My wet overalls turned cold; they rubbed against the inside of my thighs when I walked. I stood in my room, embarrassed and angry, smelling like the school toilet.

At the foot of my bed, my dolls slept in empty tissue boxes. The night before, I had given them a bath and hung their clothes over the radiator to dry. I loved my dolls and I believed that they loved me.

Every day, after school, I rushed home to play with them. But that day, I walked over to where they slept in their beds and kicked them. They tumbled across the floor and when they were still, I stepped on them roughly, until their rubber faces sank in. I could feel the warmth from the tears on my cheeks and I knew they would never like me again.

I saw Greta's shadow moving across the kitchen wall, in and out of the light. She leaned against the table, flipping through a magazine.

"Oh, look at her! She looks dreadful." She pointed to a model in the magazine. I stood, tempted to look at the photo she was pointing to.

"Greta," I said.

"Yeah?" She didn't look up from her magazine.

I held the banister. "Do you remember once you said my mother made a rule that I wasn't allowed upstairs in my shoes?"

Greta looked up at me, the magazine open in her hands.

"You made that up, you lied to me," I said.

"What are you talking about?"

"When I wet my trousers because you wouldn't let me upstairs in my boots." Even now, just saying it made me embarrassed.

"You always used to wet yourself. It wasn't my fault; you had a problem." When she smiled, the corners of her mouth curled up like a cat's tail.

I had the feeling I was holding my breath. Then I said, "I'm not surprised Trevor never telephoned you again."

At first, I thought she hadn't heard me, she stood so still. "Excuse me?" she said, raising her eyebrows. "What did you just say?"

"I said I'm glad Trevor hasn't phoned you. You're so horrible."

She dropped the magazine on the table. She stood with her hand on her hip and her lips pursed, as though she were posing for a picture. "Well, if he doesn't phone then I won't be his girlfriend. I'll be free to shag anyone I want, just like your mum does since your dad left you."

I stared at the stitching on her jeans pockets. I thought: We will never be friends again.

"My dad didn't leave us," I said, steadying my voice. "He's in India, buying antiques for the shop."

"India!" Greta said, as though it were a joke. "I just saw him walking down the King's Road."

I looked at her but couldn't speak. He was already walking through my mind, the sound of his footsteps against the pavement: a tall man with dark hair and skin, in denim jeans and a pressed white linen shirt from India. He floated down the middle of the road, his gaze somewhere between the rooftops and the sky.

Upstairs, Eden was asleep on the big bed. The room was not dark. The curtains were drawn and the light from the streetlamps shone through the windows. I looked at the things on top of Mum's dresser; I lifted the lid on the wooden apple and let it drop, the way Greta had done, humming a song.

An old photograph lay on the dresser, against the wall. In the photo, I was sitting on Mum's lap, she had her hand on my forehead, and we were both laughing. Underneath, my father had written *My two loves.*

"Eden, Eden . . . wake up." I put my hand on his shoulder and pushed him lightly. He turned over and his hand fell open on his forehead. "Eden." I pushed him again; my voice was louder. "You can sleep in my room tonight. I'll let you!" Eden opened his eyes; they were dark and wet from sleep. He sat up, rubbing his eyes with his hands. He moved slowly, stumbling forward from the bed, his forehead warm and damp from sleep.

We lay in my bed, head to toe. I pressed my toes against Eden's back to warm them. It was an attic room with a porthole window and a copper bird perched on top. A car drove down the street and the headlights crossed the bedroom wall.

"Greta said she saw Dad walking down the King's Road," I said suddenly, in the dark.

Eden turned under the covers. "Greta saw him in London?"

My teeth touched. "Yes."

"But he would have come home if he was back," Eden said. "He would have, wouldn't he? Why wouldn't he tell us?"

Eden was silent and I closed my eyes. Before he'd left, my mother and he had arguments, late at night in the kitchen and on the telephone. The morning he left for India, only Eden and I were downstairs to say good-bye.

"Do you think it really was him, May?" Eden said again, from the end of the bed.

I shook my head. "Greta's a liar."

I lay down on the pillow. I thought, Eden will never fall asleep now. He wants me to tell him Dad would have come home to us, first thing! He needs me to tell him. Then he'll lie down, turn his face to the pillow, and fall asleep, knowing he has weight. That he, Eden, is enough of a reason for his father to come home.

"Maybe it was someone who looked like him," Eden said, hopefully.

I nodded in the dark. "That's probably what happened, Eden."

"He wouldn't be here and not tell us, would he?"

"Of course he wouldn't," I said, but I lay with my eyes open until I heard Eden turn his face to the pillow, until his breathing grew soft and slow.

NINE

On the weekend, Mum and her friends Annabel and Nicole were sunbathing in the garden. They lay topless, on their backs, on bamboo mats, covered in coconut oil.

In a basket, under the shade of the tree, Nicole's baby daughter lay sleeping.

"The spirituality thing, you've always been into that," Nicole was saying, "but what more could you be looking for? You have a husband, this house. The shop's doing well. Two children."

"Are those in the good or bad category?" Annabel asked. She rested her head on a silver reflector. "I've always said, opposites attract but not for very long."

"I think you're probably right," my mother said, turning onto her stomach and resting her head on her hands.

When people asked how my mother and father met, she said that she had gone to his shop, looking for a present for a friend. The way he dressed, spoke, touched her on the shoulder made her think he was gay, and by the time she realized he wasn't, he had already seduced her.

I walked up the garden steps.

"Hello, my darling," my mother said. "What have you been doing?"

I shrugged. "Just walking around."

"That's a pretty dress," Annabel said.

I looked down, touching the tiny roses on the fabric. "Thanks."

I went over to the basket to have a look at the baby.

"Leave her, May," Nicole said, her voice like swatting a fly. "She just finally settled down."

I stepped away from the basket.

"Come lie down with me," my mother said. She moved over on her mat, making room, and I sat down beside her. I felt the sun on my back, and the straps of my sundress fell loose around my shoulders.

"You smell like the swimming pool," my mother said. "I was thinking maybe we'll go away somewhere for a week or two, just us three. I have a bit of money saved for a holiday."

"Isn't Dad coming back soon?"

"The last time he phoned he was having trouble shipping a table back." She sighed, laying her head on her hands. "Wouldn't you like to go away? You and Eden don't want to spend the whole summer in the city."

"I just want to stay here, Mum." I didn't want to go on holiday, pack the car and drive for hours—get lost, hot and bothered. I was happy to stay here, swim at the Fulham pool, and practice the breast-enlargement and stomach-flattening exercises I read about in *Sixteen* magazine.

I imagined myself returning to school anew. I had never been a good student, but I wanted for once to really try. We would be taking our A-levels soon. I had already read one of the books on the autumn syllabus. I would sit in the front row of the classroom, raising my hand and not wishing every time the teacher asked a question that she wouldn't see me.

Annabel took a joint from her handbag. "Remind me I must phone Suzy about the party at San Lorenzo's tonight. She'll put us on the list."

She lit the joint and passed it, across me, to my mother.

"I really fancy a cup of tea," Nicole said.

"Oh, so do I," Annabel said.

They sat up from their mats, tying their bikini straps behind their backs.

"Do you want some tea, darling?"

"No, thanks, Mum."

I watched them walk down the garden steps and into the kitchen. The sound of their voices and laughter floated into the garden, but I could not hear the words they were saying.

I lay by myself on the mat and wished I had friends like my mother had. Maybe from a book, maybe from a film; I had an idea of what I wanted: a friendship I had never had. I watched the other girls. Girls in twos: sitting together on the bus, walking home from school. Going over to each other's houses, spending the night. I imagined them, sitting up in their beds, talking until dawn. The light turning dark, the dark turning light, outside their windows.

When I listened to my mother and her friends talking about falling in love, I imagined a best friend, a girl. We kept no secrets from each other; our thoughts blended together in the air. She would never believe in heaven and hell but in the trees and the sky and the places hidden beneath. The color between us would be sea-green. In the secret history of friendships, engraved in stones, ours would be among the greatest. The sea glass, the pile of leaves! The friend I had always wanted. The one you were born with. That made you happy to be alive and living in this world at the same time. We were like sisters, each of us a wing of a small blue bird.

I was almost asleep when I heard the baby cry.

I sat up and went to her. A spider crawled along the wicker edge of the basket, and I gently blew it away. I put one hand beneath her head, the way my mother had taught me to do with Eden, and lifted her up.

I held her to my chest as I walked around the garden, telling her the names of the flowers and plants. "Those are daisies by the wall, and mint and thyme are growing in the pots."

Amaryllis began to cry, and I thought it meant that she didn't like me. That she could feel in me a meanness I felt in myself: a sharp bone through the skin.

Nicole ran up the garden steps. "Did you wake her?"

I shook my head. "She was crying, so I picked her up."

"Well, you should have left her. She really needs to nap." Nicole reached for her, taking her from my arms. "If she doesn't nap, she doesn't sleep well at night. You're not hungry again, are you?" she said, in a softer voice to her baby.

She sat down on the grass and unbuttoned her blouse. I wasn't sure if I should look, or look away. She put the baby's mouth to her nipple. I stood where I was, fiddling with a button on my cardigan.

Nicole looked up. She saw me watching her. "Never seen a pair of tits before?"

I felt myself blush and walked away. I had always thought she was pretty with her pale skin and round dark-brown eyes.

Nicole lay down on her side, on the mat, with the baby beside her. She closed her eyes and kissed Amaryllis gently on the forehead.

They dressed for the party in the bedroom. Annabel wore a white minidress and silver-colored sandals with long straps that tied around her ankles like a ballerina.

My mother wore a crochet vest and long dark denim skirt with wedged-heeled sandals.

Nicole sat on the bed, talking to her mother on the telephone, making arrangements to leave Amaryllis with her for the night.

Before my mother left for the party, she asked me to collect Eden from his friend George's house. George lived on Cranberry Road, just across the common.

At George's house, I straightened my dress on the doorstep.

When I rang the bell Mrs. Barstow appeared instantly, as though she had been standing behind it.

"Oh, hello!" Her voice was as high as a song. "Isn't it nice of you to help your mum, taking care of your brother. She must be quite busy alone in the shop while your father's away."

"Yes, she is, Mrs. Barstow." I smiled primly, standing with perfect posture on the doorstep.

Mrs. Barstow wore her hair back in an Alice band. Her pale-yellow summer dress fluttered in the light breeze. She was older than my mother, ten or fifteen years older, and her house was decorated like an English cottage. The print of the hand towels in the downstairs loo matched the wallpaper, and miniature seashell-shaped soaps—that looked as though they had never been used—sat in the silver soap dish.

"Eden!" she called over her shoulder, into the hall. "Your sister is here!"

Eden and George came running down the stairs. Eden held his swimming costume wrapped in his towel. From the kitchen came the smell of a roast and boiled potatoes and I lingered in the door, hoping she would ask us to stay for supper.

"Say thank you, Eden." I poked his shoulder and Mrs. Barstow gave me an approving smile.

"Thank you, Mrs. Barstow," Eden said.

Before we left, she gave us each an orange-flavored Penguin bar for the walk home.

It was a warm evening and we walked home through the common.

A woman wearing a red-and-white polka-dot dress and a man dressed in a suit sat on the bench. Couples held hands, walking along the path in the late-afternoon sun. A young boy rode his bicycle down a steep slope while his mother chased after him.

Our house was empty when we returned. The smell of Annabel's scent lingered like a ghost in the hallway.

Eden walked into the garden, calling to Porridge.

An empty bottle of white wine sat on the table with three wineglasses. Glasses with lipstick marks around the rim. I drank the leftover wine from the glasses.

A note lay on the table, beside the empty bottle. It was a shopping list:

oranges
bread
frozen peas
butter
jam

But beneath the list, hidden under the bottle of wine, something else had been written. It said, *Emptiness—what's the use of going on?*

I held the note in my hand and read the words again. I thought, A mother shouldn't leave notes like this lying around. I dug my nails into the paper.

Upstairs, I ran hot water in the bathroom sink and tore the note to pieces. The scraps of paper floated in the water. Slowly, the letters faded and the ink turned the water pale blue.

I stood in the garden. Eden had set up an imaginary game of twigs, rocks, and stones at the bottom of the tree. I thought I heard him talking to them; the sticks and stones, as though he were talking to another child.

"Eden?"

He looked at me from where he crouched on the ground with what seemed like fear—or the embarrassment of someone who thinks he is alone but realizes he has been watched.

"Have you ever heard a song that goes like this: Emptiness—what's the use of going on?"

"I don't think so. Who's it by?"

Your mother, I thought.

The evening light cut across him; lightening his face and hands. Porridge crawled out from under the bushes, she circled the terrapin pond touching her nose to the still water. Eden reached out to hold her, bringing her to his chest. "She feels so warm from the sun," he said.

For supper I made baked beans on toast and sliced tomatoes with salad dressing. Eden fed the cat leftover fish.

We carried our food into the living room, eating in front of the telly. I sipped Ribena from a wineglass, and we finished the packet of chocolate digestive biscuits.

It was Saturday night. We watched the telly until there was nothing on except lines on the screen and a girl hugging a dog. On the street outside, a woman stood alone at the bus stop, eating a packet of crisps. I fell asleep on the sofa and Eden slept on his bed of pillows on the floor.

In the middle of the night, we were woken by the sound of footsteps and our mother's voice echoing in the hallway.

"May? Eden?" she called, frantically.

I lay on the sofa in the dark room, too tired to answer.

The sitting room door flew open. "I've been looking all over for you," she said, steadying herself against the doorframe.

"You're drunk."

She shook her head and stumbled on the edge of the carpet. She held her hand to her chest. "I was so worried! Imagine what I thought when I saw your empty beds."

"Oh, God," I said, rolling my eyes. "We've slept in here before.

Where else would we have been? You were obviously too drunk and stoned to think to look in the living room."

"I'm not drunk anymore, darling. I feel perfectly fine, just a bit hungry. Should I make breakfast?"

She knelt down beside Eden. He turned on his side, pulling the blanket to his chin.

"What time is it?" I had thought it was the middle of the night, but when I looked out of a corner of the curtain it was nearly light outside. A man walked a dog on a lead. The newspapers had already been left on the doorsteps and the light from the streetlamps faded into the day.

Eden sat at the kitchen table, his eyes puffy from sleep, drinking a cup of milky tea. His blond hair stuck up like something newly hatched. The clock on the kitchen wall said half past six. The windows of the houses across the street were dark.

Our mother hummed a song to herself as she cracked eggs into a bowl: a song she must have heard at the party, a song she might have danced to. Strands of hair fell from her ponytail, around her face.

"I have something to tell you," she said.

"What is it?" I asked, my voice a flat line. I was sure it would be something bad.

"It's a surprise."

"What kind of surprise?" Eden said, his tired eyes lighting up. "Tell us, Mum!"

"Okay," she said, smiling. The smell of eggs and tomatoes filled the kitchen. "Do you really want to know?"

Eden nodded.

"We're going on holiday!" She clasped her hands in front of her, opening her mouth, so that for a moment she looked like a doll that had just come alive. Her lipstick had worn off except in the corners of her mouth, her cheeks still red from rouge and drink.

"A holiday? Where are we going?"

"That's the surprise. Guess?"

"Ibiza," I said, but she shook her head.

"Druzilla's Fun Park!" Eden screamed. He had seen the adverts on telly and had been begging her to take him. "I know! We're going to visit Dad in India!" he shouted.

Her face fell, as though popped with a pin. She shook her head, looking at Eden sorrowfully. "No, darling. We are not going to India."

She turned her back to us, stirring the eggs in the pan. A shudder shook her shoulders, and I thought, It's too early to cry this morning.

"We're going to America," she said.

"America?" I said, as though it were a word I had never heard.

"We're going to visit Renee."

Renee was our mother's friend. She had moved to America two years ago and now, when she telephoned, her voice echoed down the line. Renee had sent our mother a book called *The Beginner's Guide to Inner Peace* and tapes of Hindu chants. She kept the book on her bedside table.

The last time we went to stay with Renee, she was living with a band of gypsies on a farmer's field in Warwickshire. We stayed with her in her wooden caravan with a hot plate and a mini fridge. Eden and I slept in a cupboard under the bed, with a red velvet curtain that pulled across the opening instead of a door.

"Will we fly on a jumbo jet?" Eden asked.

"I think so, darling." She laid plates on the table, butter, and toast. Outside the day was brightening. Through the garden door I could see mist rising off the grass.

"I don't want to go to America," I said.

My mother looked up at me, as she buttered her toast. The light against her knife flashed like a sword.

"I'll stay here and take care of the cat," I said, and crossed my arms in front of me and stared at the legs of the kitchen chairs.

She let out an exaggerated sigh, dropping her knife and fork on her plate. "Why do you always have to be so difficult? I thought you would be excited to go to America. Do you know how many people would love to have this chance, a holiday? I thought you would be happy."

"Who will look after Porridge while we're away?" Eden asked.

"Greta will."

"Greta?" I said, with venom. "She doesn't even stroke her. She hates cats; they give her hives."

Mum pressed her forehead against her hand and closed her eyes. I thought, One more word and she will break. She will open her mouth and scream. She was so happy when she told us we were going on holiday; so proud of herself and of the holiday she had planned. Now I had ruined it with my questions and worries. I thought, She'll get the knives out; she'll leave the house, run down the street in her stocking feet and never come back.

"And who's going to take care of the shop?" I said.

"Oh, fuck the shop." She waved her hand in the air. "I can't be tethered to the bloody shop. Anyway, if your father cared so much about it, he would have come back when he said he was going to."

"I'll come with you, Mum," Eden said.

"Well, we'll have a lovely time together, won't we, Eden? Sunbathing on the beach in California while May stays here in the drizzle."

California, she said. California was famous; it was in songs and movies. All the film stars lived there.

"I didn't know Renee lived in California. You didn't tell us that." I kept my arms crossed, trying not to lose my frown.

But I was already planning my return. Off the plane, tanned, wearing a denim jacket, my hair wavy and bright blonde from the sun. Maybe even an American accent. A new girl, thin and confident. With something changed about me that no one could quite place: straightened like a book spine. I imagined the girls at school, flocking around me, like they do to Samantha Fenton, asking me questions about the film stars I'd met in California. A gate, separating them from me—the girl who'd been to California—so that I was admired from afar but never again involved in schoolyard cliques or gossips, never caught in a web. Yes. This would be the best part of the holiday: bragging about it in school. Already, I couldn't wait to come home.

TEN

We flew across the ocean in a jumbo jet to California. Renee met us at the airport, waving her sunglasses in the air.

"Lucy!" she called through the crowd. "Lucy, I'm over here!" They held each other tightly and for a long time. When they parted, my mother wiped her eyes with the back of her hand.

The light in the airport was glaring, like sunlight reflecting on glass. Announcements were called out over the loudspeakers, but the American voices sounded fake. They sounded like television.

In the car, Renee told us we were going to a town called Rosemont. We drove on winding cliff roads overlooking the ocean. The windows were open and warm air blew against us. The air smelled like the sea and the tar melting on the highway.

Rosemont was a two-hour drive from the airport. It was not on a cliff overlooking the ocean but in a canyon. Renee and Mum were talking in the front seats, laughing and smiling, as we drove across a rust-colored bridge. The wind and the sound of the cars on the highway made it difficult to hear the words they were saying. I closed my eyes. They felt dry from the airplane, and the sun was too bright, making me feel unbalanced and awake. Eden sat next to me, looking out his window.

We turned off the highway onto a two-lane road. Renee looked back at us, "How's it going back there?"

Her skin was darkly tanned, which made her teeth look surprisingly white when she spoke. Her dry chapped lips made her seem thirsty, even as she sipped water from a plastic bottle.

In London, Renee had been known for her eccentric style. She would wear colored striped tights with a gypsy skirt, high-heeled boots, a leopard-printed shirt, and a cowboy hat. "By some minor miracle," Annabel would say, "it all comes together." She had been overweight and always trying new diets she cut from the pages of magazines. I remember coming home from school and seeing her in the kitchen, beating her thighs with wooden spoons to get rid of the cellulite.

Two years ago, before she left London for California, she helped her elderly mother sell her flat and move into an assisted living home in Brighton. She was her mother's only child, so this was her responsibility. At the home in Brighton, her mother had a nice room, with a short walk to the shops. Renee had not been back to England or seen her mother since.

The houses in the canyon were built of wood and painted brown. Trailers were parked in rows in lots. A torn couch sat in the driveway of a house. A baby in a playpen watched her mother water the lawn. A man fixing his car turned to look at us as we drove past.

Renee pulled into a gas station. While she filled the car we went into the convenience shop, and our mother bought us each a Coca-Cola and a packet of American crisps.

Even in the canyon, the sun seemed too bright: hot, pressing down against the tops of our heads and on our skin. We drank our Cokes through plastic straws and wandered around the convenience shop, looking at the American things: pink bubble gum, Pixy Stix, baseball caps, suntan lotion, FOR RENT/FOR SALE signs in neon orange.

Mum and Renee sat on a bench outside. Mum sipped a ginger ale and smoked her last cigarette. Renee drank a seltzer. "This is the closest shop," Renee told her. "It's where you come if you need to make a phone call or are desperate for a fag."

While they talked on the bench, Eden and I wandered over the parking lot to the edge of the woods. The trees in California were a reddish color, tall and thin. They were not wide and stout like the trees in England. One tree had been used as a place to put chewed-up chewing gum; its entire trunk was covered in it. Of all the trees, what bad luck to be this one.

Cigarette butts and beer cans littered the ground. Dried pine needles covered the earth, and the air smelled faintly of smoke. In the car, Renee told us that it hadn't rained in weeks. There was a drought and fires were burning in the forests all across California.

We turned down a dirt road and stopped before a set of mesh metal gates. A man appeared from behind the gates, waving to Renee. He unlocked the chain and motioned us to drive ahead.

A sign inside said WELCOME TO THE PARVATI ASHRAM.

Renee explained that to leave or enter the ashram you must have permission from Parvati. "Once you've been invited here," she told us, "no one ever wants to leave."

Renee parked and helped us with our luggage. We followed her along a sandy path that led farther inland between the trees. The air was dry with the scent of sun and wood. A twig caught beneath the strap of Eden's sandal, and burrs stuck to his socks. A large winged insect flew by and I covered my hair with my hands, worried it might get caught. That had happened to me before, in the loo at school, when a spider had fallen on my head.

As we walked, Renee put her arm around our mother. "I'm so happy you're here," she said. I saw our mother's face flush from the compliment.

"I'm glad to see you too," she answered, but the words sounded awkward.

We came to a large clearing in the woods, where several houses stood. Beyond them, like a stone in the center, was a deep blue pond. "It's beautiful here," our mother said, looking around her.

"Parvati's followers purchased the land about seven years ago and built the houses and the temple on it," Renee said. "See, everyone who lives here pays a monthly rent, depending on their income. The rich pay more, the poor pay less. All people who live on the ashram are assigned a chore, like cooking or cleaning, even gardening. Some people have jobs outside, in the neighboring towns. I used to work in the kitchen, but now I'm in training to be one of Parvati's Women." Renee gripped my mother's arm with excitement.

"I see," our mother said, her voice full of air.

"It's like a large family and Parvati is the mother," Renee said, smiling at Eden and me.

We came to a large wooden house. Renee rang the doorbell and we stood on the stone steps, waiting in the shade of a palm tree. Bright flowers and waxy green plants had been planted around the house, and the grass looked green and soft, despite the lack of rain.

A woman answered the door. "I'm Keshi," she said, taking our mother's hand in hers. "It's so nice to finally meet you. Renee has told us so much about you. Welcome home."

Keshi was a tall woman with dark skin, eyes, and hair. She wore a white sleeveless blouse and long skirt. She made me think of an island.

She led us through a large empty room with stained-glass windows and brown carpeting. "This is where darshan is held," she said. She led us through the house and into the kitchen.

We sat down at the table, and she offered us a plate of sliced apples and oranges, sprinkled with coconut. She poured us each a glass of water and offered to make us tea.

"Keshi," Renee said to us, "is one of the Women."

"Oh, really?" Mum's eyes went back and forth between Keshi and Renee.

The Women, Renee told us, were the closest people to Parvati. They lived in her rooms, cooked and brought her all her meals, and helped to advise her.

"Ladies in waiting," Renee said jokingly.

Keshi brought cups of tea to the table, and I could smell the mint and steam rising from them.

The sun shone through the windows and sliding glass doors. In the distance we could see the dark blue pond, glistening under the sun.

"Mum"—Eden tugged at her shirt—"I want to go swimming. You promised us when we got here we would go for a swim."

"Let me just finish my tea and then I'll take you."

"Oh, they'll be fine on their own," Renee said. "All the children swim by themselves. You don't have to worry. And I know Parvati would like to see you alone."

I saw my mother glance at her. This was one of the things that irritated her the most: when her friends who didn't have children told her what to do with hers.

"Mum, you know I'm a really good swimmer. I already have my trunks on under my trousers."

"Will you go with him, May?"

I nodded. The sun in the kitchen and the warmth from the tea was making me feel tired and dizzy.

"Oh, all right, you two, go and have a look," she said. "But May, don't let him go in by himself."

We stood up from the table. Renee opened the door for us, and Eden and I stepped outside onto the flat stones. When I looked back, I saw our mother watching us, as she sat at the table in the bright kitchen with Keshi and Renee.

"Come on, May," Eden yelled, eager to get to the water. "Whoever gets there first is the winner!" he shouted, as he ran toward the pond.

"The winner of what?"

Two yellow and black butterflies flew by me. One landed on my shoulder, and I raised my arm to make it fly away but it stayed, closing and opening its wings, not afraid. They were larger than the butterflies in England, whose wings were so thin you could see through them. As delicate as pressed flowers, you were afraid to touch them. These butterflies had a thickness, their yellow and black wings beating like bees.

Eden kicked off his sandals, stepping down the slope to the water. "It's so warm," he said, turning to look at me. "It's like a bath."

Mud floated up from the bottom, mud and tiny black fish. I stood in the warm water, looking at the houses, the acres of neatly mowed lawns and planted flowers.

A man wearing shorts and no shirt, his hair pulled back in a ponytail, pushed a wheelbarrow along the path. Small birds flew above us, crossing the pond from treetop to treetop. For a moment everything went silent: the birds made no sound and the man pushing the wheelbarrow made no sound, as though I were watching from behind glass.

I lay back on the grass, thinking about how far we had traveled. Eleven hours on the airplane; we had never been this far from home. I imagined I could see a bridge in the sky connecting us. A map, a string to follow, that would lead us home.

As I sat up, I saw three girls sunbathing on the wooden dock across the pond. A girl wearing a red bikini stared in our direction, shielding her eyes from the sun.

"What's your name?" she called. At the sound of her voice, the two other girls sat up, rising sleepily from their beach towels.

"Me?" I touched my collarbone. "My name's May."

"What?" she yelled back, louder. Now she stood with her hands on her hips at the edge of the dock.

I tried again. "May!" I could hear my voice disintegrate across the water. When I thought of returning from California to my school in London, I imagined this part of me would be gone. A shyness, a voice that couldn't reach the front of the classroom, frozen in the loo stall afraid to pee, while Samantha Fenton and her friends waited in line outside.

The girl in the red bikini stood at the edge of the dock. In one sweep, she raised her arms above her head and dove into the water. The other two followed, diving in after her.

Eden stepped back from the water's edge. "Let's run!" His voice repeated in my head—*let's run, let's run*—but we stood on the grass watching them.

The girl in the red appeared first, wading toward us thigh-high in the water. "Hi," she said. "I'm Sati."

The water fell from her like rain, sliding down her tan body, landing on the grass. She was tall and thin with small breasts and a waist just starting to form. Her shoulder-length brown hair clung close to her face.

"I couldn't hear what you said your name was," she said, wringing out her hair. Her voice sounded softer as she walked closer. She had a pretty face and green eyes. Freckles covered her nose and cheeks.

"My name's May."

"May? That's a nice name. Where are you from?" She stood next to me, the water dripping from her body onto the dry grass.

"London. I just arrived," I said, not looking at Eden, as though he might somehow magically disappear beside me.

The two other girls emerged from the water, making their way onto the grassy bank.

"This is Summer and Molly," Sati said. Summer had dark skin and eyes. She wore her hair in two long plaits to her waist. There was an awkwardness in the way she stood, slouched over, bending at the shoulders. The way girls who grew too fast, towering above the boys, stood hunching in the class line.

"You have a funny accent," Molly said. She stood beside Sati, adjusting the top of her yellow swimming costume.

"I like your accent," Sati said, looking at me. She turned the rope bracelet on her wrist. "We're going to see the horses. Do you want to come with us?"

The horses grazed in the field and the girls stood at the fence watching them. The sun was in the middle of the sky and the sky was pale blue. After a while, the girls went into the stables, and Eden and I followed them. They walked barefoot over the prickly grass, pebbles, and stones and sat on the haystacks in their bathing suits.

Sati lifted the lid from a barrel of oats and Molly and Summer gathered around. Eden and I sat next to each other on the hay bales, watching them pick out pieces of dried dates and coconut from the horse feed.

"Have you met Parvati yet?" Summer asked.

I shook my head.

"You'll probably get to meet her tomorrow," Sati said.

"Oh."

As I watched them, I felt too nervous to speak. I felt the hay prickling against my legs.

"Do all of you live here?" I asked, then suddenly thought it was a stupid thing to say.

"Yes," Molly said, in a tone that said *Of course we do*. "But I've lived here the longest. My parents moved here before Parvati was famous."

In the car, on the way from the airport, Renee had told us about Parvati's recent notoriety. She had been interviewed on television and in newspapers all over the world, because of her work with young men who were dying from AIDS. She was not afraid to touch and hug the sick and dying, while the doctors stood at a distance in masks and plastic gloves.

Now, on the ashram, she had built a hospice. It was filled with young men, her disciples, who were suffering from AIDS.

"What exactly is a guru?" I heard Eden ask.

The girls looked at each other, but none of them answered. Molly shrugged. "A guru is a guru."

"Parvati is a holy person," Summer said. "She knows God. God talks to her and tells her things. God sends messages that only she can hear."

I nodded. "Oh, I see." I said, as though it were perfectly clear. Turn right, turn left—the directions to a street.

There was a sound at the stable door and the girls hurried to cover the barrel of oats, leaning back on the hay bales as though they'd been lounging all day.

Two teenage boys walked in; one pushed a banana-seat bike.

"It's only Dylan and Brad," Sati said, as she pushed herself off a hay bale. "They're brothers."

"Hey, Sati," the boy with the bike said. "I bought you a present."

Sati crossed her arms. "Whatever it is Brad, I'm not going to kiss you again. Your braces cut my lip."

"Sorry," Brad said. "I'm getting them off in a few months."

He pulled out a Snickers bar from his shorts pocket. It was squashed, but Sati didn't seem to care.

"Where did you get that?" she asked excitedly.

Brad smiled. His metal braces flashed on his teeth. "We've got our sources. We're already on a sugar high." He held out his hand and his brother fived him with a giant leap off the haystack.

"Thanks, Brad," Sati said, as she opened the wrapper. The chocolate had melted and now stuck to her fingers. She licked the chocolate off.

"Can I have a piece?" Molly asked, holding out her hand.

Sati broke off small pieces, giving one to Summer and one to Molly.

"Open your hand," she said to me. I saw Eden watching her, wondering, hoping he would be offered some. She put some candy in my hand and I brought my hand to my mouth.

When she placed her hand in mine, I noticed a gold ring she wore with a small ruby.

"That's a pretty ring," I said.

"It's my wedding ring," she said. "I'm married to God."

"Yeah, but God's celibate," Brad said, smiling slyly. He leaned against the wall. He looked about sixteen, lanky in camouflage T-shirt and cut-off denim shorts.

"Well, Parvati married me to him," Sati said.

"It's my turn next," Molly said. "Parvati said she would make me one of God's brides when I did better in school."

Dylan climbed the wooded beams of the barn, into the hay loft, and sat up there watching us.

"Come up here," he called to Summer, who looked at him shyly.

Sati stood beside Brad. "Thanks," she said, kissing him on the cheek. She leaned her head against his shoulder. Her hair had dried and was light brown, falling past her shoulders. The sun coming from the windows made her green eyes look as though there were pieces of gold in them.

Later, we left the horses and followed them to the dining hall. They walked from the stables and sat at the tables in their bathing suits and bikinis, barefoot. A sign outside the door said, PLEASE REMOVE SHOES. I left my sandals on the rack with the other shoes, but all through dinner I worried someone might steal them. They were purple wedged sandals, and I bought them with the money I'd made babysitting Eden.

The dining hall was a large wood-paneled room with a cathedral ceiling. There was an excited, secret feeling inside, the way I imagined boarding school would feel, or a summer camp in the woods.

The sound of voices rose to the ceiling, with the constant clink of dishes, the scrape of knives and forks against china, and laughter. The windows were open, and warm sweet-smelling air filled the room.

Across the dining hall, I saw my mother sitting at a table with Renee; they were talking and laughing. Renee covered her mouth with her hand. Eden and I carried our trays toward her, but we could see that her table was full.

Sati touched my shoulder. "I saved seats for you next to me."

We followed her to a round table in the middle of the room and put down our plates. Dinner that night was salad, brown rice, sweet potatoes, and a bean and tomato stew. Eden touched his food with his fork, prodding it.

A man carrying a tray of food passed our table. "How's my sweetheart?"

"Fine, Dad," Sati said, blowing him a kiss as he walked away.

I recognized him from before. He was handsome, in a square-featured American way, the way I imagined the pilot who flew our airplane or an American doctor would look. We had seen him on the path when we arrived, and Renee had told us that he was a millionaire, the richest man on the ashram and one of Parvati's favorites. He had raised the money for the hospice and the new school building.

Sati's father set the tray of food down in front of a woman sitting alone at a table.

"Is that your mum?" I asked.

Sati nodded. "She's going to have a baby," Sati said. She crossed her fingers in the air. "Please God—I mean, Parvati—let it be a girl. I hope it's a girl," Sati said, holding up crossed fingers.

"I was hoping my mum would have a girl too," I said. "But it was a boy."

Eden looked at us from across the table, his fork near his mouth. "Mum told me when I was a baby you used to dress me up like a girl and push me around in my pram pretending I was your baby sister."

Sati thought this was funny and laughed aloud. She took a sip of water.

"Can you keep a secret?" she said to me.

I nodded, but I had never been able to keep a secret for long.

"My mother's going to give the baby to Parvati."

"Why?"

Sati shrugged. "As a gift."

I looked at her but did not know what to say.

"Parvati has always wanted a baby," Sati said, "so my mother said she would give her one."

I looked around the room for my mother. I wanted to go to her, to sit beside her, but she was surrounded by people. She held a mug of tea in both hands and her cheeks were flushed. She looked pretty and young; her hair fell loose around her face, and her eyes shone brightly. She smiled at something one of the men at the table said, tilting her head back so the arch of her teeth showed. I realized that I hadn't seen her laugh like that in a long time.

We were given a room in Hanuman House, a small room with a window that looked out to the woods. A bed took up most of the space. A set of sheets, towels, and a blanket lay folded in a pile. The room was painted white.

At night, Mum hung a shawl over the window, so the sun wouldn't wake us too early. She lit a candle that had been left, half melted, on the windowsill.

The bathroom was shared by everyone on the floor. A note taped to the mirror read, *Be considerate of others. Leave the bathroom the way you would like to find it. Namaste.* These kinds of notes were posted all over the ashram.

We brushed our teeth and wiped the sink clean with a piece of toilet paper, then carried our toothbrushes and toothpaste back to our room, where we kept them in a cup on the shelf. The house was sparse, tidy, and clean.

"What did Parvati look like?" I asked our mother when we were alone in our room.

"She's from India," she said. "She has long black hair down her back. She was dressed in a green sari and had a red dot in the middle of her forehead. She wore about a hundred gold chains around her neck and enormous diamonds, the size of ten-pence pieces, in her ears."

The three of us sat together on the mattress with a blanket over our knees. It was a warm night but we sat close, talking about the guru in low voices, because the house was full of strangers and they were devoted to her.

"How old is she?"

"Maybe in her late forties. I'm not sure."

"What can she do?" Eden asked impatiently. "I mean, can she cast spells? Can she make things float or move them with her mind?"

"Maybe she can, but we just talked."

"What did you talk about?"

"We talked about"—I felt her squeeze my hand—"relationships and love, things like that."

"Mum," Eden said, "the food here is horrible."

"The food is rather dull," Mum agreed.

"My stomach hurts. I didn't eat anything for dinner."

"Pass me my handbag," she said, nudging me with her elbow. She rummaged through it and pulled out four pieces of cheese wrapped in red wax and some packets of crackers and peanuts she had saved from the airplane.

"I took them from the man's tray next to me," she said. "He slept the entire flight."

We divided the cheese and crackers into threes and Mum pulled out a roll of Rollos from her handbag.

"Mum!" we said, excitedly reaching for them.

We sat huddled together, with Mum between us. Eden laid his head on her shoulder and she stroked his hair. This feeling was familiar; it reminded me of an earlier time I couldn't place exactly: a secret knitted-together feeling.

"So, all these people live here just so they can be near Parvati?"

"Yes. She's their spiritual teacher," Mum said. Eden and I looked at each other and started to laugh. We laughed when Mum sang the hymns too loudly in church and we laughed when she said the words, "Making love."

"How do you know she's real and not just pretending?"

"I felt it," Mum said. She held her hands in the air as though she were molding the words. "She makes you feel this warmth, this kind of love when you're near her. She makes you feel taken care of, like everything will be all right."

There was an expression on my mother's face, a glazed look in her eyes.

"Can she do any magic, like make herself invisible?" Eden asked.

"Eden, she's not a witch or a sorcerer, she's a spiritual teacher!" I said, laughing so hard Eden began to laugh too.

"Really, you two. Laurel and Hardy."

"But seriously, Mum," I said, when I had calmed down, "why does she get to be the guru? I mean, what's so special about her?"

"If you stop talking and giggling, I'll tell you the story."

A story. We settled down on either side of her to listen. "A long time ago—well, not too long ago," Mum began. Her voice was soft, and a breeze came through the window. "When Parvati was a young girl, six or seven, she woke up one morning and said to her father, 'I want to meet the Maharaji.'

"'Why do you want to meet the Maharaji?' her father asked her. So she told her father she'd had a dream about him, the same dream every night for over a year. In the dream, she sat at Maharaji's feet, and he gave her a cup of rose water to drink.

"Eventually, Parvati's father agreed to take her to see Maharaji. It was a long journey; they had to travel by train. When Parvati met Maharaji, she knelt by his feet and would not leave. She put flowers on his bed; she prepared his food; she washed his clothes and refused to return home with her father.

One day, while she was washing his clothes in the river, she saw blood in the water. The blood was coming from her hands. Maharaji told her not to be frightened; the blood on her hands was a sign from God. She had stigmata.

"What's stigmata?" Eden asked.

"It's like the marks Jesus had in his hands when he was nailed to the cross," our mother said.

Eden looked frightened. He held his hands together as though even the mention of this was enough to cause him pain. In London, we had watched the story of Jesus on television and it made Eden cry, watching Jesus carry the cross through the crowds, the thorns on his crown cutting into his forehead.

"It's all right, darling," Mum said, kissing him on the side of his head. "She's very kind and warm, not frightening at all."

Eden nodded. He laid his head against her chest and closed his eyes. The story was over and the candle burned low on the windowsill.

The flame flickered as we lay down to sleep, and our mother kissed us good night and blew out the candle. I kept my eyes open. The night outside the window was lighter than the room, and the shape of the trees appeared through the shawl. The shadows of the branches looked like hands against the wall. They made me think of blood in the water.

ELEVEN

In the morning, the sun shone in the room. Eden was still asleep; so was Mum, with the pillow over her eyes. I went to the window to look outside. The sky was clear and the trees looked crisp in the light.

California. We were in California.

A young boy, who looked about Eden's age, ran down the path toward the house. He ran quickly, barefoot, holding a letter in his hand. I heard footsteps up the stairs, then knocking on the door of our room. Mum sat up with a start. "What is it?"

I opened the door and the boy was standing there. "I have a message for Lucy from Parvati," he announced. "Parvati wants to see you and your family this morning."

His ribs rose and fell as he caught his breath to speak. He must have been no more than ten years old, but there was a fierce expression in his eyes, which seemed too old for his body. As though his own eyes had been taken from him and replaced with the eyes of an old man.

Parvati's house was surrounded by a high bamboo fence, so that no one outside was able to see inside to her private gardens.

We were escorted by Renee. She led us down the passageway to a room with a red carpet where a small group of people were gathered.

"Lucy and her children are here," Renee said, from the doorway.

The people in the room turned to look at us. I saw Sati's mother and father sitting in the crowd.

Parvati sat above them, on a daybed. There were pictures of her in all the houses and rooms of the ashram, so I was not surprised by her appearance. She looked the way our mother had described her to us.

Her long dark hair fell around her. She wore a bright-green silk sari. Her face was elaborately made up, with eye shadow, lipstick, and mascara. There was a red dot in the middle of her forehead.

She looked at us from across the room. "Come here," she said. We followed our mother through the room to her.

"I want to see the girl first," Parvati said.

"Go on, May," My mother said, pushing me lightly between the shoulders. "Don't be afraid."

I looked back at her, embarrassed that she had said this aloud. Parvati took my hands in hers. "May." She held my wrists tightly. "Your mother has told me you can be difficult. Look at me." She put her hand beneath my chin, turning my face to hers. "I can see that you are unhappy. Tell me why."

I shook my head, fighting back tears. "I'm not unhappy," I said.

She held me tightly in her arms. "Who has hurt you?" she said quietly, in my ear. I felt myself begin to cry and I clenched my teeth to stop. I hated my mother then for bringing me here, to cry in front of a roomful of people.

Parvati put her hand on the back of my head. "It's all right," she said. "Everything will be all right."

I wiped my eyes. I felt myself flush from the embarrassment of crying. I'm just tired, I thought, tired from the airplane.

"Your mother has come a long way to be here with me," Parvati said. She is very brave. Most people do not have the courage to leave what they know. You must learn to respect her; she loves you very much. Do you understand?"

I wanted to pull myself away from her, to run out of the room, but I nodded like a puppet.

"She has given you so much. She's been a mother since she was nineteen, and now she needs you to be strong for her. Will you do this? Promise me."

"Yes," I heard myself say.

She called Eden to her. "You are a sweet child," she said to him. "Your soul is pure, but your mind is not. This is something you must fight against in your life."

Eden, a pure soul. I imagined the color of green sea glass.

Eden glowed from the compliment. A gold star. Parvati kissed him on the cheek. Then told us to say good-bye to our mother. She needed to talk to her alone, and children were not allowed in the room anymore.

Eden and I stood outside, in the shade of a palm tree.

"Where should we go?" Eden said.

"I don't know."

We walked along the path, between the rows of trees.

Parvati was like a movie star, I thought. In her room there was a glass case full of ornate perfume bottles arranged on a tray. Through a half-open door in the hallway, I saw a dressing table and mirror surrounded by small white lights.

The day Keith Richards came into our father's shop to buy an Indian chest for his German stereo, Sebastian went breathless. He practically fell over himself, trying to help him. My father played it slightly more cool, but even he was flustered: too busy with him to answer the telephone or help the other customers in the shop. It reminded me of the way Parvati's followers treated her—too eager to please. In the room, when she had asked for a glass of water, there was a moment of panic among the disciples, as though her request couldn't be granted fast enough. As though they feared no water could be found.

Eden and I walked along the path. He looked at the ground, kicking up sand with the toe of his sandal.

"I think Parvati's a liar," Eden said loudly. I pulled him by the arm. Two men with shaved heads were walking up the path. "Namaste," they said, as they passed. By the way they smiled at us, I was sure they had not heard what Eden had said.

In the car from the airport, Renee had told us the ashram rules: no sex, drugs, or alcohol. But the major rule was this: If you knew of someone who had broken a rule or spoken badly of Parvati or the ashram, you were expected to tell on them to Parvati or the Women.

"What do you mean, Eden?" I said, when the men were gone.

"Well, I was looking at her palms, but she didn't have any marks like Jesus. She didn't have any marks at all."

"Are you sure?" I looked down at the sand. Why hadn't I thought to look at her hands? Was Eden becoming smarter than me?

"Well, I think so." His voice sounded vague and he bit the nail on his pointing finger.

"You think so or you know so?"

"Um—well, I think we should try to have another look."

That afternoon, Eden and I sat hidden by a hedge in the shade, chewing on blades of grass and breaking up little twigs. We were devising a plan called How to Get a Really Good Look at the Guru's Hands.

Later, we went to Parvati's house and knocked.

Keshi opened the door. She smiled at us but did not say anything.

"We came to see Parvati."

"Yes."

"We have a very important religious question, concerning God," Eden said, "that we need to talk to Parvati about."

Keshi told us to wait a moment while she went inside.

Eden and I waited on the doorstep. I looked at him and smiled.

The door opened. Keshi held a plain piece of paper. It waved gently, like a sheet on a clothesline.

"Here you are," she said. "You can write your question on the paper and drop it in the box by the door. Namaste."

We wandered around the ashram, thinking of what to do next.

We saw Renee at the temple, making a picture from different-colored rice. The picture, she told us, was of the Ganges River in India. Parvati had asked her to make it from a photograph she had. It reminded her of her childhood.

"We were wondering," I said. "How do you get to see Parvati?"

"Take her a present," Renee said, half jokingly.

"A present?"

"When I wanted to see her I would give her one of my rings." I looked at Renee's hands; her fingers were bare. In London, she wore rings on every finger, sometimes three or four, and each ring had a story.

"This ring," she would say, touching a small rose-colored diamond, "belonged to my great-grandmother. This one I found in Hyde Park on my way to work yesterday morning."

"Why did you give Parvati your rings?" I asked.

"So that I could see her in her rooms. Parvati loves jewelry, and she needs gold to keep down her Shakti."

"Her what?" My voice creaked like a door.

"Her Shakti," Renee said clearly. "She needs to wear gold to stay grounded to the earth. Otherwise she would float away to God."

I imagined Parvati, in her green sari, unlatching each gold chain from her neck, pulling the gold bangles from her wrists, growing lighter and lighter, a cool smile on her face, as she rose above the treetops and through the clouds, disappearing in the sky.

Eden and I sat outside the temple, watching Renee finish the rice picture. Inside the temple was a statue of Hanuman. A plate of sliced fruit lay at his feet. On the temple wall was a poster-size photograph of Parvati sitting outside with her disciples around her.

Renee finished the picture, but as she stood to leave, a few grains of blue rice fell into the yellow sun. "Oh, God damn it!" she said, hitting her fist against her forehead.

A small fire burned in a pit. It was called the *dhuni,* and all day and all night, Renee told us, someone had to watch over it, making sure it continued to burn.

Parvati liked presents and she needed gold. In our room, I held my mother's gold chain with a glass locket in my hand. "We can't give this away, it was her mother's," I said. "And besides, she promised to give it to me for my eighteenth birthday."

What else did we have? Eden's drawing book, the last three titles in the Famous Five series, sun lotion, and shampoo. I had my silver butterfly earrings, but she only liked gold.

We lay on the mattress on the floor, looking up at the ceiling. The room was warm, the window was open, but no air came through. It suddenly occurred to me that if God knew everything, wouldn't He see us scheming? And if Parvati knew God, wouldn't He tell her about our plan? I panicked, imagining the spell she would put on us: bread crusts and a rusty cage, the key thrown away.

"What if Parvati gets suspicious? What if she knows this is a trick?" I said to Eden. "If she does have powers, she might punish us. Aren't you afraid of that?"

Eden shrugged. "Not really."

I stared at his little face. "Why are you so annoying?" How could he be so casual and watery when I had to pick the fallen leaves from the pavement lines. Skipping over the cracks; a cross, a kiss; count to ten and start again. In my dreams, there was a man in a black van, slowly following me along a deserted road.

"I know what we can give her," Eden said, suddenly jumping up from the bed. He rummaged through the pockets of his rucksack and pulled out a small box. Inside the box was a gold coin from China, a good-luck charm in a plastic box, and it was gold—or at least it was the color of gold.

"Let me see." I reached for it, but Eden closed it in his hand.

"I'm going to give it to her," he said.

I went to the mirror to brush my hair. Eden wiped the box clean with a handkerchief and spit and put it into the front pocket of his shorts.

"Come here, Eden, you've got knots in your hair." I held the hairbrush by the handle. Eden stood with his hand covering his pocket, looking at the door. Before he could escape, I grabbed him and parted his hair to the side. "You look much better now," I said, and tucked my shirt into my denim skirt. Then, looking quite businesslike, we went to the guru's house.

Keshi opened the door of Parvati's house.

"We have a present we would like to give Parvati," Eden said.

Keshi smiled and held out her hand. "You may leave it with me."

We explained, at length, how the gift had come from China, to London, and then to California, safely, in our carry-on luggage, so there was absolutely no chance of losing it in the baggage claim, which is why it was so important that we give it to her ourselves.

Keshi told us we could wait inside. Eden and I sat on a wooden bench in the hall. Two ceiling fans turned above us. A woman vacuumed the brown carpet in the room on the other side of the doorway.

An older man sat on the bench across from us. He stared down at his feet, with the ashamed look of a child who has just been scolded.

We sat quietly on the bench for what seemed like an hour or more, before Keshi led us down the long hallway, past a series of rooms, and outside to Parvati's garden.

Parvati sat in a lounge chair by the side of her swimming pool. A tray of iced drinks with lemon and mint leaves sat on the table beside her. She sipped her drink while Eden and I stood quietly, waiting for her to notice us.

Two men sat on chairs beside her. One of the men strummed a song on the guitar. He had curly shoulder-length hair and a necklace made of Rudraksha beads. We had seen him the night before in the dining hall, and Renee told us he was the son of a famous American folksinger.

A girl swam in the pool by herself; it was Sati. She waved to us from the turquoise water.

"You have a question for me?" Parvati lifted her sunglasses to her forehead.

"We brought you a present," Eden said.

"A present?" Parvati said. "Oh, I love presents!" She raised her hands in the air and the gold bangles on her wrists fell together like a chime. The two men looked over at us, squinting in the sun.

Eden held out the coin, wrapped in a handkerchief. Parvati looked at it as he held it in his hand; then she reached for it, turning her palms upward. There was nothing on her hand, only the lines across her palms and the backs of the gold rings on her fingers. No scars from nails, no scars at all. He put the coin in her hand and she closed her fingers around it. "Lovely children from England," she said again, but there was nothing there.

*   *   *

There was nothing there! Eden and I ran back to our room, excited and half afraid, imagining the collapse of the ashram, the revolution, once we had spread the news. We closed the door and sat down on the bed to catch our breath. Where was our mother? We needed to tell her what we had found out. We needed to tell her right away.

As the sun set behind the trees, Eden talked excitedly about his discovery: the gold coin from China, her up-turned palms, that he was the first one to think to look at the guru's hands.

The day grew dark. I had a nervous feeling in my stomach. We ate the leftover crackers from the airplane and drank a plastic cup of orange juice with a foil cap. Outside we could hear dinner being called. We had left the window open with the light on inside, waiting for Mum, and mosquitoes filled our room.

The day was ending and my cheeks burned from the sun. I lay under the covers with a damp towel across my forehead, feeling the way I had when I was six and in bed with scarlet fever.

During the weeks I was in bed in a darkened room with scarlet fever, I read a book about a group of friends who discover a passageway into another world. The story turned into my dreams. In my dreams, I went with them into the secret world, where everything was covered with snow but never cold. There was a message one of the children told me, a riddle hidden in a song. The words made the shape of a golden key, the key to the other world, but the dream always ended too soon and I awoke, stranded in my bed, straining to hear the rest of the words.

Today, we had discovered the guru was a fake, but instead of gloating, like I did when I found my mother's lost watch in the flowerpot, I stared up at the ceiling with a cold, hollow feeling inside. There was no magic in this world.

We were asleep when our mother came back to the room. She stood in the dark, watching us.

"Mum?" I said, sitting up.

"Shh," she whispered. "You'll wake Eden."

"Where have you been? We've been waiting for you."

"I've been with Parvati," she said slowly. Her voice was as clear and still as her body. Like a glass. It was the way she sounded after she had been crying and after she wiped her eyes, rinsed her face with cold water, and looked at herself in the mirror with a new clarity.

"What were you doing with her?"

"She's helping me figure out some things in my life."

Eden turned under the covers. "Mum," he said. "Is that you?"

"Yes, darling. Try to go back to sleep, I didn't mean to wake you."

She began to undress in the dark. The air lightened around her and her body darkened against it, so that her arms and legs, even the expression on her face, became visible.

"Mum," Eden said, sitting up in bed, "we made a discovery today."

"What is it?"

"Parvati doesn't have stigmata," he said excitedly. "We went to look at her hands, and there was nothing there."

She stood still, her hand on her shoulder. She stared at us on the bed, as though she were listening but could not understand what we were saying.

"What are you talking about, Eden?"

"We went to see her today. Renee told us to take her a gift, so we spent all day trying to think of what to give her and I found the gold coin from China in my suitcase." Eden spoke quickly, as though time were running out, telling her about our plan.

"You went through all that trouble just to look at her hands?"

"There was nothing there! Not one little scar," Eden said, his voice growing louder. "That means she's lying about having the marks of Jesus."

Our mother dropped her skirt to the floor and stood naked in the dark. She pulled her hair back from her forehead and held it with her hands. "The marks aren't always there; they come and go. She is not a fake, I promise you. All these people wouldn't be living here if she were. Why are you two always so suspicious of everyone?"

I sat up, confused that this news hadn't meant more to her.

"Why don't you believe us?" Eden asked.

She shook her head, as though she had had enough. "Why can't I have just one nice day? Why can't I have just one day for myself without hearing this kind of nonsense from you? Don't you ever trust me? Don't you trust what I'm doing? Don't you know that everything I do is for you, to make sure you feel loved? I never felt loved by my mother."

She looked suddenly at the window, covering her bare chest as though a person had appeared in it.

"What, Mum?" Eden said, looking to the side at the open window.

Our mother sat down on the edge of the bed and pressed her palms to her eyes.

"I'm sorry, Mum," Eden said. He put his hand on her back. "We just thought maybe she was pretending."

After a while she lay down beside us in the bed, placing a glass of water on the floor beside her. She leaned across me, kissing my cheek, then Eden's too. "Let's try to go back to sleep now. It's been a long day for all of us."

TWELVE

In the morning, we met Renee for breakfast in the dining hall. While Mum and Renee were talking, I noticed Eden looking across the room at a young boy who was sitting alone at a table.

"Darling," Mum said to Eden, when she saw where he was looking, "why don't you go over and make friends with him? He looks about your age."

Renee turned in her seat, looking at the boy. "His name's Jabe," she said. "He moved here a few months ago from Los Angeles." Renee leaned forward, speaking quietly. "He's very shy. His mother used to leave him alone in the apartment when she went to work because she couldn't afford a babysitter. She left him a pile of sandwiches and two glasses of milk and the television on while she worked a double shift."

"Oh," Mum said, glancing at the boy once more. "Eden, come on. Let's go over and talk to him." She stood up from the table, taking Eden's hand, walking cautiously across the room. Jabe had straight brown hair and large round brown eyes. Even now, as he sat at the table alone in a room full of people, he looked toward the door, as though he were waiting, hoping for someone to arrive.

"Well, I have to go to my chores," Renee said, as she stood up, clearing her plate from the table.

Sati and her mother walked into the dining hall. Sati wore her bikini top and denim shorts, her hair pulled back into a high ponytail.

She walked across the room and sat down in the chair beside me. "Parvati liked the present you gave her," she said.

"She did?" I said, surprised at the excitement in my voice.

"What are you doing after breakfast?"

"I don't know." I could smell her grape-flavored lip gloss.

"The girls are meeting at the pond."

Sati's mother carried a tray of food to the table. She set a bowl of yogurt and raisins down in front of Sati.

"When's your baby due?" my mother asked, when she came back to the table.

"The end of November." Sati's mother smiled, touching her belly. "I'm Caroline," she said, reaching out for my mother's hand.

"I'm Lucy."

"You just arrived. Is this your daughter?"

My mother nodded. "And that's my son over there."

"He's sweet. I love their accents."

My mother watched Eden, who was showing Jabe the set of playing cards the stewardess had given to him on British Airways.

"Looks like he's found a friend," Caroline said.

"I hope so." My mother smiled at her.

"What house are you in?"

"We're in Hanuman House. All three of us in one room."

"The three of us spent almost a whole year in one room. That's when we decided to build our own house."

"Your own house?"

Caroline sipped her water; she put her glass down on the table. "It's the gray house off the path."

"Oh," my mother said. "I was wondering who lived there."

"We needed a little privacy and more room."

"How long have you lived here?"

"Almost four years now," Caroline said.

My mother looked at her, waiting to hear more. "So, how do you like it?" she said, hunching her shoulders slightly.

"We've been happy here," Caroline said. "In fact, our lives have changed. When we first met Parvati, my husband's business was bankrupt, our marriage was falling apart, and Sati was doing terribly in school, but since we've been with her everything has turned around for us."

My mother smiled at her.

"It's not all easy. John—my husband—and I are apart a lot. He has to commute once a week to Denver, stays for three or four days, then flies back for the weekend. It's tiring for him."

"I can imagine," my mother said.

Sati ate her yogurt; she swung her legs under the table. "Can we leave now?"

"You didn't eat much," her mother said, looking into her bowl.

"I'm really not hungry."

"Where are you going?" my mother asked when she saw Sati take my hand.

"We're just going to the pond," Sati answered.

"Don't forget to put on your suntan lotion or you'll burn," my mother said. "The California sun is much stronger than the sun in England."

"I won't forget," I said.

Summer and Molly were sunbathing on the dock when we arrived. Molly lay on her back with her Walkman on, singing aloud to the song playing in her ears. Summer lay on her side, reading a book.

I spread my towel out next to Sati's.

"Do you want me to put lotion on you?" Sati asked.

"All right, thanks."

"When I first came here I got such a bad sunburn there were blisters down my arms and I had to go to the hospital."

"The hospital?" I said, as though it were a dangerous word. In London, I saw a man, standing alone outside of the hospital, weeping. Even now, when I thought of him, I wondered what had happened: his wife dying, his mother or father, his child?

I lay on my stomach with my head to the side. I heard Sati squeeze the lotion into her hands. It felt cool as she rubbed it into my shoulders and down my arms. I closed my eyes and felt her hands move from my ankles up the back of my legs to my thighs.

"Open your legs a little bit," she said, into my ear. Her hands moved beneath the elastic of my bathing suit, in between my thighs. As she moved her hands back and forth I felt a warmth between my legs. It was the same feeling I had in bed at night when I thought of the boy Nicholas in Scotland.

As we lay on our towels in the sun, Summer, Molly, Sati, and I went around in a circle, asking each other questions. Who is your favorite actor? What's your favorite book? Favorite band? Each time a new question was asked, I hoped my answer would be the same as Sati's.

Suddenly, Molly screamed. A small black insect was crawling up her arm.

"Just stay still. It's only a spider," Sati said, as she scooped it up in her hands.

Molly made a face, "It might be a black widow. They bite, you know."

"Parvati says we're not allowed to kill bugs. It's bad karma," Summer said. "Except mosquitoes. That's self-defense."

"I would never kill a spider anyway," I told them. "Spiders are good luck. Haven't you ever heard the tale of Robert the Bruce in the tower? He was inspired by a spider spinning her web."

"Whatever," Molly said.

"Let's find a safe place for the spider to make a web," Sati said. "Where it won't get stepped on accidentally." At first I thought she was talking to all of us, but then I realized it was just me. She wanted me to go with her.

I followed Sati across the grass and into the woods, looking for the perfect tree, one with low branches away from the path where people walked. When Sati found the tree, she placed the spider on the bark and we watched as it crawled quickly up the trunk.

"It'll make its web, up there," I said, watching it. I wondered how long it would stay in this tree.

When I looked back at Sati, I realized she had been watching me. Our eyes met and I felt a flicker, like the flame on a matchstick, that our friendship had struck.

Sati said she wanted to show me the grapefruit grove. We walked past the houses and the pond, out to the field where the horses grazed, and beyond the stables to a shaded grove. In the grove, the trees were planted in long straight rows, and pale yellow grapefruits hung from the branches.

Sati stood on an empty wooden crate and pulled herself up into the tree so she sat straddling the branch with her legs. She picked a grapefruit and handed it down to me.

"Thanks," I said, looking up at her. I held the fruit in my hands, and it felt warm from the sun. I had never had a grapefruit right from the tree before. I'd tasted honeysuckle off the stem, and berries from the field, but the only grapefruits I'd had came wrapped in cellophane from Sainsbury's.

I dropped the skin to the ground. The fruit inside was watery and ripe, the sections breaking apart in my hand. When I bit into a piece, the juice ran down my chin.

"These are delicious," I said to Sati. "They don't taste like the ones from the supermarket."

Sati pulled one off the branch for herself. She climbed out of the tree and we sat with our backs against the bark, eating the fruit. The smell of the grapefruit mixed with the smells of grass and sun.

"I've never heard the name Sati before," I said.

Sati picked the white skin from the grapefruit. "Parvati gave me my name when we moved here."

"Oh," I said. "Does she give everyone a name?"

Sati shook her head. "Just some people."

"What's your real name?"

Sati looked up, confused, "You mean the name my parents gave me?"

I nodded.

"Alice."

I looked at her and thought, Her name was Alice.

"When you go home, do people still call you Alice?"

Sati shrugged. "I don't really go back to Denver anymore. I mean, I've only been once, when my grandmother was in the hospital."

"Are your grandparents still alive?"

"Yes, but I haven't seen them in three years."

"My Grandmother Hannah died last year," I said, "but I think about her all the time. Especially when I walk past the places she used to take us. I don't think I'll ever stop thinking about her."

She looked at her hands. "I used to miss mine too, but I made myself stop thinking about them. When we first came here I wanted to go home so badly I would steal money from my father and walk all the way to the gas station to call them from the pay phone."

"The gas station with the shop?" I thought of the place we had stopped with Renee on the way from the airport, but it seemed as though it was miles away.

"Yeah," Sati said. "I'd leave early in the day, and it would take an hour or more to walk there."

I thought of Sati walking along the highway alone, with the cars and the sun: the road smelling of tar, the cars passing.

"You walked all the way on the road?"

Sati shook her head. "Not on the road. Someone would have seen me. I followed the stream at the end of the grove through the woods. But someone found out what I was doing and told Parvati."

"What did she do?"

"She told me I wasn't allowed to leave the ashram again. That was the last time I spoke to my grandparents. They drove here to see me once, but no one let them in," she said.

"They came all the way and you didn't see them?"

"No one told me they were here." She leaned her head back against the tree, squinting up at the sun.

I imagined her grandparents, sitting in their car. Her grandmother looked like the older American women I had seen in the airport: overweight, in pastel colors and white ankle socks and white sneakers. A cooler, a hand-held fan, a map that had been unfolded and refolded on her lap. Waiting in the car, sweat forming beneath her legs against the leather seats. Sati's grandfather walking up to the locked gate. Calling out to Alice. Calling her name over the gate. Her grandmother would look away. The smell of the canyon air, the deserted road; she would think the worst things. Things she had seen on television about cults and gurus.

"It's all right," Sati said. "Now I don't want to see them anymore. I don't want to leave or go anywhere else."

"What do you mean?"

"Because I know now, that this is where God wants me to be." I looked at her.

From where we sat we could see the trees at the far end of the grove and the sun shining above them cast a yellow-orange glow.

Sati reached forward, gently wiping a drop of grapefruit juice from my shirt with her hand. "When we were younger we built a fort over there. We don't use it anymore," she said, "But now the younger kids do."

I looked up at the sky. There was no breeze that I could feel, but the clouds moved swiftly across.

Sati grew quiet. "Oh, listen. Do you hear that?"

"Hear what?"

"Wait." She put her finger to her lips.

I held my breath and heard the sound of bells in the distance.

"The bells are ringing. That means there's darshan tonight," she said.

"What's darshan?"

"It's when Parvati comes out and talks to everyone."

Sati stood up. I didn't want to leave our spot in the grove. I felt tired from the walk and warm from the sun.

"Come on," she said. "If we don't get there early we won't get a seat near Parvati."

She reached for my hand, pulling me up. I didn't want to leave, I didn't care about a seat close to Parvati. I wanted to stay here, talking to Sati in the shade of the grapefruit trees.

Darshan was held in a large room in Parvati's house, with brown carpeting and windows that rose up to the ceiling overlooking the pond. The room was lit only by candles and the paler light of the moon through the windows.

Sticks of incense burned on altars. Fresh flowers stood in vases. A daybed, where Parvati would sit, had been made up with orange and red silk fabrics and large pillows. A glass of iced tea, with pieces of lemon and fruit floating in it, waited on a tray with a single flower. I would spend most of the evening watching Parvati take sips from the drink and wondering what it tasted like.

Renee was hovering nervously around the daybed, arranging and rearranging the flowers and pillows. Keshi came in, carrying a vase of yellow roses. "They arrived just in time," she said, as she set them down on the table.

They were not the wildflowers that grew in the surrounding fields; these yellow roses had been ordered and delivered by van from a florist's shop. Like Sunday at church, everyone had dressed up a bit, the women in floral sundresses or blouses with skirts and the men in dress shirts and trousers. They sat on meditation pillows, waiting for Parvati to arrive. Everyone on the ashram came to darshan, even the babies and young children, who fell asleep on the floor with their heads in their mothers' laps.

A man named Krishna Das began to play the harmonium, and Peter Runyun played the hand drums. A thin Indian woman sat straight-backed, with her eyes closed, hitting a small brass cymbal. The roomful of people started to sing an Indian song. My mother leaned over and whispered the name of the song into my ear. It was called the *Hanuman Chalisa*. It was a prayer to the guru.

Soon, everyone stood and the chanting grew louder. The door to Parvati's rooms opened and she entered surrounded by the Women.

"My *chelas*," Parvati said, as she walked through the crowd, blowing kisses, touching hands, "I love each and every one of you."

A great cheer sounded in the room, rising like the tone of the cymbal. The devotees' faces shone, like people in love.

Parvati took her seat at the front of the room and said she would lead us in a meditation to connect us with our luminous self, the self we were born with. With her as our teacher, she told us, we had the opportunity of reaching enlightenment in this lifetime. We had escaped the trappings and temptations of the outside world. We had been chosen. Guided—by God—to be with her.

She asked if we had any questions before the meditation began. A man near the front of the room raised his hand.

"Yes, my Thomas," Parvati said lovingly, the way a mother might speak to a young child.

He sat on a meditation pillow with his back straight and his hands on his knees. He looked as though he was in his early thirties, with a boyish face, short blond hair, and a white-collared shirt buttoned to the neck.

"My pride," he said, "is getting in the way of my devotion."

Parvati looked at him. "Your pride?" she said. "What have you got to be proud of?"

For a moment Thomas appeared stunned, punched. Then everyone laughed and he relaxed, laughing along with them.

A pretty woman sitting near Parvati raised her hand. Her name was Kelly; she had long light-brown hair, a small sloped nose, and freckles. Earlier that day Sati had pointed her out to me. She said Kelly had had an affair with one of the men on the ashram, and as punishment Parvati made the man leave and they were never allowed to see each other again.

"Parvati," Kelly said, "I'm trying so hard to forget about Michael, but I still feel heartbroken. . . ." She paused, and I thought she might cry. "The pain of missing him feels unbearable at times."

"The pain is unbearable?" Parvati said to her. "Go to India. See the children begging on the streets. Children with babies begging on the streets. Look at those children and then tell me about your broken heart."

When there were no more questions to be answered, Parvati said we would begin the meditation. I saw Sati close her eyes so I closed mine. I wasn't sure how to meditate. Was it a prayer, or a string of wishes? But Parvati told us to let go of the thoughts that came into our mind: to have no thoughts at all and focus only on our breath.

I could not think of nothing. I concentrated on my breath, but different things still came into my head. I remembered a day when I was eight or nine and we were staying by the sea in Scotland. It was not a warm day. I had gone for a walk by myself, late in the afternoon, and I sat down on rocks where the waves broke. The tide was coming in, and in the distance the line between sky and sea was turning to one color. The waves crashed loudly against the rocks and a wave crashed against me, soaking my clothes. I knew that one large wave or rush of water could pull me in, but I wasn't afraid.

In my pocket was a fifty-pence piece, and I threw it into the sea. I made a wish—a wide wish—for all the people and for all the animals in the world. A wish for the sky and sea. A wish for everyone to be happy. I sat on the rocks, staring at the waves until the sky turned dark, and I felt the air blowing through my skin and through my bones, but at the same time I felt as though a light were shining out from me, shining out from the center of me.

When the meditation ended, it seemed as though a weight had been lifted from the room and calmness had settled in its place, lying down like a great sleeping cat.

That night, after the meditation, Parvati picked a flower from the vase. She said a short prayer in Hindi, kissed the petals, and tossed the flower into the room.

The flower landed in my mother's lap.

An older man, with tired-looking eyes, raised his hand. "Parvati," he said, trying to steady his voice, "I am ready to give you my heart."

In the darkened room, I saw my mother nod, looking up at Parvati, as though she were saying, I am ready to give you my heart too.

Afterward, we rose from our places slowly, quietly, as though waking in a roomful of sleeping people. As we were leaving, I saw Sati standing outside the doorway of Parvati's room, asking Keshi if she could go inside.

Most of the people left the room, but a few remained, still sitting on the floor, like the last guests at a party. The candles had burned low, the incense had turned to strings of ash. A small flame on a candle flickered inside a red glass vase. When I hear the word *loneliness,* when I see it written in a book, I think of that room.

Outside, our mother was talking to Renee and Caroline. She held the stem of the flower, like a candle, between her hands.

"It's a sign," Caroline whispered to her. She held her hands on her belly, her dress falling like a tent around her.

Renee nodded, looking down at the flower my mother held in her hands.

"I felt a peacefulness that I've never had before," I heard our mother say.

"The teachings grow even deeper," Caroline said.

"The beginning is often the most blissful time. Later, as you dig deeper it can be more painful. Right, Caroline?" Renee said. The two senior girls.

Eden and I stood next to each other, waiting for our mother to finish her conversation. There was a rustle in the crowd and a small woman with a high-pitched voice pushed her way through. "Excuse me, please. Excuse me," she was saying.

The woman made her way toward Eden and me.

"May? Eden?" She said, pointing the end of her pencil at us.

"Yes." I touched my collarbone. "I'm May."

I didn't know the woman's name, but I had seen her before, putting up notes in the houses, approaching people in the dining hall with her pen and clipboard.

"Well! I've been trying to find you two all day. I really need to talk to you." She spoke so quickly I could barely break the words apart. "You haven't been doing your chores, you know, and when chores aren't done the whole place becomes a mess."

"I didn't know we had chores," I said.

"Everyone who lives here has a chore. How do you think things get done? It's not by magic."

"Well, we don't live here. We're just on holiday." I said.

Her eyebrows rose from behind her glasses. "Holiday? This isn't Club Med."

She studied her clipboard, pressing the rim of her eyeglasses to the bridge of her nose. "Let's see what we have for you. . . . Okay. May, you are working in the stables taking care of the horses, and you, young man, will be in the vegetable garden."

"The vegetable garden?" Eden said. "I hate vegetables."

"Well, you're gonna learn to love them, sweetheart." She wrote down the times and places of our chores on index cards and handed them to each of us. "They start tomorrow. *Capito?* Be on time and do your work well. I don't think you'd be happy cleaning toilets, would you?"

As we walked back to our room, our mother told us that she had been assigned a chore too: cooking for Parvati in the kitchen of her house. She cradled the flower in her hand. The moonlight reflected on the dark pond, as she looked up at the sky. "Wasn't I lucky? Of all the places to land, the flower fell in my lap," she said, half joking and half amazed.

Like a coin flipped, a turn of luck: It was a sign that this time we had come to the right place. This time she had made the right choice, and behind her the past mistakes turned golden: the house by the sea, the fights with our father, the things that had upset her were the things that had brought us here, the stepping-stones that had led us.

THIRTEEN

Our mother stood on the dock, in her long skirt and short-sleeve blouse, a straw hat on her head, watching Eden and Jabe row a small wooden boat to the grassy bank.

"He's so happy here," she said as she watched them. Her words sounded like a song. Her voice rose and her face flushed when she saw that we were happy. A toy at Christmastime, a kiss on our forehead, anything that made us smile.

"May, you're looking a little red; don't forget to put the sun lotion on."

"I'll make sure she does," Sati said, smiling at me.

The lunch bell sounded through the ashram and my mother looked at the face of her watch. "May, will you make sure your brother eats lunch? And please put some more sun lotion on his back."

I sighed, looking up at the sky. "Why don't you do it? You're his mother," I said, mostly for Sati. I saw her back shake with laughter, as she hid her face in her towel.

"May," my mother said, sounding hurt, falling, as though I had ruined her moment on the dock, watching her happy son. "Remember what Parvati said? She asked you to help me while we were here. Please, May," she said again, looked at her wristwatch and rushed away barefoot, across the dry grass to the storage room, to get the flour for the cake for Parvati's five-o'clock tea.

In the dining hall, I sat beside Eden, making him eat the kale and whole wheat spaghetti.

Before Sati and I left for our chores, I slathered sun lotion on Eden and accidentally got some in his eyes.

"See," I said, in a goody-goody voice as we walked to the stables, "I'm helping Mum with Eden, just like Parvati asked me to."

"Parvati can see too," Sati said. "She sees everything."

"From where?" I had an image of her perched in the trees.

"God tells her."

When Sati talked about Parvati, it was as though she had been swept away; she was seeing me and talking to me from the circle of another world, a world where Parvati was as definite as the sky and the sea.

Sati stood in the field, brushing a brown horse named Boxer. "Every day," she told me, "we have to give them fresh water and put clean hay in their stalls."

She wore her red bikini top, navy-blue dolphin shorts, Dr. Scholl's, and nothing else. She led me around the stables, showing me where to put the brush and tack. The water and feed. The clean hay. The apples and carrots. She told me the names of each of the horses and stroked their soft noses.

When we had cleaned, watered, and fed the horses, we went inside the stables to sit in the shade and rest. I told her that we'd missed breakfast and she poured me a paper cup full of cool water and gave me a grapefruit. I thought of Eden in the vegetable garden and wondered if anyone had offered him a glass of water or anything to eat.

Sati lay back on the hay bales and fanned herself with her hand. "I asked Parvati to give you this chore," she said.

"You did?"

"It's one of the best ones. Only the Jewels get it."

"What are the Jewels?" I said.

"The Jewels are Parvati's favorite people, and everybody wants to be one."

"Oh," I said. I sat across from her, with my back in a spot of sun.

"Do you have a boyfriend?" Sati asked.

"A boyfriend?"

The question surprised me, like walking into a glass door. Boys weren't interested in me. My mother and her friend Annabel, even Greta, promised me that I was pretty, but they said not in a way that boys my age would see. "When you're older," they said.

I knew what I lacked: a tartness, a tease, a fun-loving flirtatiousness. There were girls in my form, Samantha Fenton and Sheba Marks, who had boyfriends, and everyone knew they were not virgins. I watched them—while I pretended to wait at the bus stop outside the school gates—with their uniform skirts rolled up to their thighs, smoking cigarettes and flirting with the older boys from the grammar school across the street.

"So, do you?" Sati asked.

I wasn't sure whether or not I should lie. Maybe she thought of me as a Samantha Fenton.

I shook my head. "No, but there's a boy I like in Scotland. Do you have a boyfriend?"

"Sometimes Brad and I fool around, but it's not much fun. I had a boyfriend in Denver; he was older. He was fun."

When I imagined an American girl, it was Sati. Strong and thin, singing the words of a song; confident with boys and confident with girls.

"Why was he fun?" I pressed my hands beneath my thighs, into the hay bales. I had worn my favorite T-shirt and denim miniskirt. I knew Sati worked in the stables and I had dressed up a bit for her.

Sati shrugged. "He knew what he was doing," she said.

The light from the window fell against her, so her body was in the sun but her legs were still in the shade. "Do you want me to show you what he used to do to me?"

"All right." I thought she would tell me the details, the way Greta had told me about her boyfriends, or draw a picture in the dry sand: a diagram.

Sati stood up. "Come up here," she said, as she climbed up to the hay loft.

I followed behind her, up the ladder.

In the hay loft, she stood facing me under the low beamed ceiling.

"Lift up your arms," she said.

I lifted my arms above my head. She stepped toward me, took the bottom of my T-shirt, and pulled it over my head. She dropped the shirt on the floor by my feet, then pulled down the shoulder straps of my bra.

"Oh," I said, not expecting this. I took a step back.

She placed her hands on my breasts, cupping them. Then she held my nipples between her thumb and finger, gently turning them until they grew hard. At first I stood, unsure of what to do; no one had ever touched me like this.

She took my hand, pulling me to the floor. "Lie down," she said. I lay down on my back, looking at her. She put her mouth onto my nipples, sucking first one and then the other. Then she undid her bikini top and put her face to mine, kissing my mouth. I put my hands on her breasts, touching them the way she had touched me. Her breasts were smaller than mine, firmer, her nipples almost brown. I felt her tongue in my mouth. I had kissed boys before, but still I was not sure how or if I kissed well. I remember feeling swallowed by them, but Sati's lips were the same as mine and this kiss felt gentle, tingling.

Then she lay down beside me, looking up at the wooden ceiling. I remember feeling stunned, watching the dust rising in the sun.

Sati sat up. She pulled her bikini top back on and made her way down the ladder. I could hear her below, humming a song to herself.

After a while I sat up. I felt unbalanced, as though I had just stepped from a boat to shore. I took my time, unsure of what I would say when I saw her. When I looked at my chest, my nipples were bright red. I held the palms of my hands against them for a moment, before getting dressed and going down the ladder.

My mother, Renee, and Caroline stayed late over tea and dessert, talking in the dining hall. The women on the ashram loved to talk about Parvati—her hair, her jewelry, the outfits she wore—as though she were a movie star.

Renee said that when Parvati came back from India last year with her nose pierced, half the women on the ashram rushed to the piercing and tattoo parlor at the Jackson Mall, requesting a diamond stud, only they didn't have diamonds at the Jackson Mall; instead, they had rhinestones in plated silver that gave them all infections.

When Richard, a famous hair stylist and devotee of Parvati's from Los Angeles, gave her a fashionable short haircut, many of the women and teenagers took a photograph of Parvati with her new haircut to Sizzors, the local beauty parlor.

Parvati's clothes were handmade of imported silks from India. They were shipped to her in boxes covered with colorful stamps. Her disciples gave her the diamonds and gold she needed to keep her grounded to the earth. For her birthday, Sati's father had given her a strand of diamonds that was rumored to have cost over five thousand dollars.

After they had talked about Parvati and my mother talked about her troubled relationship with my father, their next favorite subject was motherhood.

Renee had never had children and did not hide the fact that the subject bored her. She would often excuse herself when the conversation turned to Caroline's pregnancy and children, and leave to join another group in the dining hall.

Caroline told my mother of the advantages of raising children in a close community like the ashram. She said that when Sati was young, she remembered feeling so lonely and depressed during the day, at home in the suburbs of Denver. The house, she felt, was like a stone around her she could not move. But here she never felt lonely, and since all the cooking and chores were shared, she never felt overwhelmed by housework.

My mother told her of a dream she had once, when I was a baby and she was exhausted. She was nineteen and a new mother, the shop had just opened, and Simon could not afford to take any time off from work to help with the baby. When he came home he still expected dinner to be ready and the house to be clean.

Just before dawn, after being up for hours during the night, she fell asleep and dreamed that fairies had flown in the window and were in the kitchen, scrubbing the pots and pans, drying the wineglasses with a tea towel. The dream was so vivid, she said, that when she woke and went downstairs to the messy kitchen—the sink still full of last night's dishes, dirty glasses still on the table, the floor unswept—she burst into tears.

While our mothers talked late in the dining hall. Brad and Dylan gathered all the kids on the ashram to play a game of Capture the Flag. They announced themselves captains, and each took turns choosing who would be on their team. They picked the girls they liked first—Brad picked Sati, Dylan picked Summer—and Eden and Jabe and the other younger children were chosen last.

We ran barefoot around the grass, until 10 P.M., our curfew, when we had to be back in our houses. We would fall asleep in our swimming suits and wake up the next morning and start the day over again in the swimming suits we had slept in.

I spent the days with Sati. Eden spent the days with Jabe and the other boys, fixing and rebuilding the fort in the grapefruit grove. In the afternoon, when we were done with chores, we would all meet at the pond. Eden and Jabe, Brad and the other older boys, Sati and I, Summer and Molly. We swam and lay in the sun, flicking away the horseflies, until it was dinnertime and we would walk to the dining hall in our swimming costumes and sit down at the tables.

My skin burned and peeled, burned and peeled again, and finally turned brown. I lost track of time; the days somersaulted into each other. I didn't want the summer to end. This was the best summer holiday we had ever had.

Sati and I lay on the grass at the edge of the pond in the late morning sun. I was staring at my arm, watching the water drops evaporate, when I heard a woman's voice.

"Hi, girls!" It was Kelly. "Enjoying the last days of summer vacation? School starts Monday, you know."

Kelly stood in front of us. I saw her calves and pretty sandaled feet with coral-colored painted toenails. She wore a T-shirt that said BROWN UNIVERSITY across the chest and a denim skirt.

"School's starting Monday?" Sati whined. "I don't want the summer to end yet. Can't we have just one more week of vacation?"

Kelly laughed. "One more week? It's already the middle of September; all the other schools have already begun."

"It's the middle of September?" I said. The sun shone brightly in my eyes as I sat up.

"Yep," Kelly said. "And remember, no bathing suits or gum chewing allowed in my classroom." She waved good-bye to us and walked away.

It was the middle of September! There had been no change in the weather; not one leaf had fallen from the trees. The sun was as constant as a light left on.

Our father would be back from India by now, working in the shop. My school in London began last week, and Mrs. Jenkins had warned me that if I missed any more time I would be left behind. I pictured the girls with their holiday tans talking about their summers in the school courtyard.

Sati stood up, shaking out her towel. "I can't believe the summer is over," she said again. "We better go to chores now."

"I have to find my mother," I said. I felt a panic begin, ticking inside of me.

"What's wrong, May?"

"I didn't realize how long we had been here. We have to go back to London."

Sati looked at me. I thought, for a moment, that she would cry. "I don't want you to leave," she said, taking my hand in hers. "Please don't leave yet. Maybe Parvati will let you live here. She doesn't let everyone stay, only special people. I can ask my dad to ask her."

"Live here?" I had never thought about *living* here; it was so far away from home. "We can't live here," I began to say. "My father's in London and our house . . . we have a cat . . . and my grandfather's getting old. . . ." I said the words, but they sounded too simple, like pictures in a children's book.

"I missed my home at first too," Sati said.

"I have to tell my mother," I said.

"I won't tell anyone that you're not going to chores."

"Thanks, Sati."

"I'll see you at dinner tonight," she said, as she slipped on her Dr. Scholl's and made her way across the grass to the stables.

I ran to our house and up the stairs into our room, but my mother wasn't there. I stood in the room, looking at the bed and the walls, at the clothes hanging in the closet, thinking, We have to go home.

The sounds of splashing and shouting came from the pond, and in the spaces between the trees I could see Eden and Jabe cannonballing off the dock.

"Eden!" I called, but he did not hear me. The light fell in pieces through the branches. I stood for a moment watching them, laughing and shouting and splashing each other in the water.

I ran to Parvatis house. Through the glass doors, I saw my mother in the kitchen, cooking with Keshi. I tapped on the glass, waiting for one of them to notice me. They were talking, mixing dough in a bowl. The radio was on and neither of them heard me. In the light of the kitchen, my mother looked happy and carefree—talking with Keshi, opening the oven, laughing with her hands on her knees.

I tapped louder on the glass and my mother turned around to see me.

"May?" she said, looking surprised, as she pulled open the sliding door.

"Mum, I need to talk to you."

"Is something the matter?"

"Yes."

"What is it?"

"I need to talk to you alone."

Keshi turned from the stove, a mitt on her hand. "We're just in the middle of making Parvati's tea." A bell timer sounded, and Keshi pulled out a rack of apple turnovers and placed them on the counter to cool.

My mother looked at Keshi. "Keshi, the next batch won't be ready for twenty minutes. I'm just going to get some flour from the storeroom."

Keshi sighed. "I'll watch the pastries and make the jasmine tea," she said, sounding annoyed.

"I won't be long," my mother said, as she wiped her hands on her apron.

Outside, the sun shone down on the flat stones. I saw our reflections, standing there in the sun, as she closed the glass doors.

"What's the matter, darling?" my mother asked, when we were away from the house.

"Do you know that it's already the middle of September?"

She looked at me but did not answer.

"Aren't we going home?"

She looked to the left, staring out over her shoulder. "No."

"What do you mean?" I heard a crack in my voice. "What happened to our airplane tickets?"

"They've expired."

I had a feeling that I was being pulled down, suddenly, under the waves. My mother put her arms around me, "I'm sorry. I was going to talk to you and Eden tonight. Parvati said we could stay here, and I think it's a good idea."

My mother reached for me, stroking a loose piece of hair from my eyes, but I hit her hand away and she flinched.

"You said we were only here for a holiday!"

"I know, but you and Eden seem so happy here. You get to spend so much time outside and you've both made friends. You don't have to listen to your father and me arguing. Parvati says staying here is the best thing I can do for my children."

"She doesn't know," I said. "I want to go home."

"Don't you like it here? What about Sati? Won't you miss her?" Her voice, I thought, had a slant—a needle pulling a thread. Had she seen us together? Had she seen us standing too close to each other, face-to-face in the pond, one of us with our eyes closed? Had she seen us touching each other beneath our beach towels as we lay on the dock, thinking no one was watching?

I looked away, at the pale green grass. I would miss Sati; I would miss her so much. She was the only reason not to go home.

"How long are we going to stay here?"

My mother shook her head. "I'm not sure. Let's see what happens."

"A week?"

"I don't know."

"Does Dad know?"

"Yes."

From the doorway of the house, Keshi called my mother's name.

"I have to go now," she said. "We'll talk about this later. May, please don't tell Eden. I should tell him myself. All right?"

From the doorway, Keshi called her name again.

"'Bye, darling," she said, kissing me lightly on the cheek. She turned away from me, walking quickly and then running up the stone steps to the kitchen.

I watched my mother disappear through the doors. I felt the sun on my back and shoulders, warm and heavy. I could not believe we had missed our flight home. That the day had come and gone, that the airplane had left without us. I imagined our names being called out over the loudspeakers in the airport and our three empty seats in a row. What had I been doing? Sunbathing with Sati. Eden running to the fort with Jabe. And our mother had known. Had she looked at her wristwatch, thinking, The flight is gone?

When we first came here I imagined what the ashram would look like to my father. The grounds were constantly being tended to, the temple and houses repainted. The trees, the bright green leaves, and the flowers were always in bloom—flowers that would cost one pound fifty a stem from the florist. I thought, looking around as though seeing it for the first time, He might think it is beautiful here, he might actually like it, which made me eager for him to come.

He would see our mother, suntanned and relaxed, laughing with her friends. We would sleep in the small room together. Maybe Parvati would cast a spell around them—a golden circle, a ring—and they would fall in love like they did when they first met.

But inside the houses was a smell of sulfur in the water mixed with the stale smell of incense, which had seeped into the furniture and wall-to-wall carpet. The kitchens were old, with linoleum floors and the counters were stained.

The first time my mother left my father, before Eden was born, we went to live in a house in Shepherd's Bush that had been converted to flats. An old man lived below us with his small dog; it was his house, and his wife had recently died. Sometimes I would go to his place and he would make tea, open a packet of biscuits, and let me watch the afternoon telly. He was a kind man, but too old to sweep the stairs or repaint the halls, where the paint fell like snowflakes from the ceiling.

There was only one bedroom, so I slept behind an antique screen in the living room. My father came to see me on Sundays, his visiting day. One Sunday the bell rang and I answered it without thinking. I had forgotten he was coming and was still in my nightgown, playing with my dolls on the floor by the radiators. I had been watching cartoons and drinking warm milk with Ribena since dawn.

He stood in the doorway, in his navy winter coat. "Did you forget about me? I've got the car double-parked on the street."

I shook my head. "I didn't forget." I hurried to get dressed behind the screen.

When I came out, he was standing in the living room.

"How can she live like this?" He bent down where the ceiling sloped. The small kitchen table was covered with wineglasses and

teacups, the purple syrup of the Ribena had spilled onto the table in
a sticky puddle, and the ashtray was overflowing with gray ash. I hoped
he wouldn't see my fingerprint in the ash. It had looked so soft that
morning, so much like the finest sand, I had to touch it. I could still
see the mark and smell the ash on my fingertip.

There was an expression on my father's face, around his mouth,
as though he were standing in the cold. I followed him down the
stairs to the street.

In the car he rubbed his eyes with the palms of his hands. I
knew he was crying and looked away. He didn't understand why
my mother had left him and the house they had just bought, in an
up-and-coming neighborhood. A house with three bedrooms and a
small garden. Why had she left him? For what? To go and live in a
tiny one-bedroom flat? Why had she chosen this over him? It was
like looking into a mirror and seeing nothing.

I knew what I would do, if he came to the ashram. I would
show him the horses. His father was a bookmaker and the horses he
knew belonged to rich men, men who were driven to the races in
Rolls Royces and Bentleys. I wouldn't tell him these horses had been
rescued from local farms and the slaughterhouse. I would tell him
they were Thoroughbreds and he would be impressed.

I walked along the shaded path. I felt the small rocks and burrs
beneath my feet, but they didn't hurt anymore. I thought, I should
have known. I should have known we would be staying here and not
going home. There had been signs: the yellow flower that landed in
our mother's lap. And the rose-gold locket that had belonged to her
mother—the locket she had promised to give me for my eighteenth
birthday—she had given to Parvati one night in darshan.

On my way back to our room, I passed the ashram office. This was
where rent checks were dropped off, donations made, and bills paid.
I noticed that the door had been left open, but there was no one

inside. A woman named Shiva was the office manager; she always kept the door locked and the key with her.

I touched the handle, pushing it lightly. "Hello? Shiva?"

The sky was not yet dark. The light came through the windows of the office. The computer had been turned off, the lights had been turned off, but Shiva had forgotten to lock the door. I called her name again, and when I was sure she was not there, I picked up the receiver of the telephone. I was going to call my father.

It had been many weeks since I had last used a telephone, and now it felt strange and heavy in my hand. I realized, suddenly, that the receiver was warm as though someone had just been holding it and I turned around, looking behind me.

A can of lime-flavored seltzer and a packet of salted pretzels closed with a rubber band lay on the desk. I pressed O, for the operator. I couldn't decide where to try first, my father at home or at the shop. Too flustered to count, I heard my heart beating in my throat.

When the operator answered, I told her I wanted to make a call to London, England. I was speaking softly, cupping my hand in front of my mouth. She told me to hold while she connected me to the international operator.

While I waited, holding the phone to my ear, I saw a photograph of Parvati on the wall in front of me. It was a photograph I had seen many times before. The photograph hung in all the houses, but in this one it looked as though she were behind the photo, looking at me through cut-out eyes. I put the telephone down.

As I ran out I had the feeling Parvati was following me, a close over-the-shoulder feeling. Not the way I imagined God would watch me—far away and from the sky—but as though she were invisible, right behind me, stepping in my footprints in the sand.

When I got back to the room, Mum was there with Eden. He showed her the drawings in his notebook while she sat on the bed beside him, listening to him explain each one. She had brought us two whole-wheat apple turnovers left over from Parvati's kitchen.

I knew she had not told him yet, and I stood in the room with the door open behind me.

"Has Mum told you yet?"

My mother looked up at me. "May."

"Told me what?" Eden said.

"Please close the door," she said to me. "Eden?"

"What, Mum?" He looked up at her as he ate the pastry, the crumbs falling on his drawing book.

"We're going to stay here for a while."

He looked up at her but did not say anything for a moment. "What do you mean?"

"I mean that we're not going back to London right now."

In the plain light of the room, the fullness of Eden's face broke and he began to cry.

"Oh, my darling," Mum said, the coolness of her voice evaporating as she held him in her arms.

"This means I'm going to miss George's birthday party," he moaned into her shoulder.

I felt myself smile. A pinprick in Mum.

"Oh, Eden," I said. "And you have been looking forward to his party for so long."

Eden shuddered. The sympathy gave his tears a new strength. He leaned into his mother's shoulder, burying his face from the news of leaving his house and father again.

"George's mum was going to bake a cake and decorate it like a swimming pool," he said, taking in a wobbly breath. "With marzipan water and little people swimming in the lanes."

Mum sank into him. I could see the sorrow on her face. Her sweet boy, and she had made him cry.

"I'm sorry, darling," she said. She reached for his hand and pulled him to her. "I'll make you a cake shaped like a swimming pool one day," she said, and Eden laughed.

"You never make cakes like that, Mum," he said.

"Well, I'll buy you one from the store and pretend."

"All right. I already know which one I want for my next birthday," he said.

"Do you?"

"Yes. I do."

She kissed his cheek, looked at me and smiled, and reached out to touch my hand. "It'll be all right, darling," she said. "I promise you. Let's just try it out, and if you're not happy here we'll leave. All right?"

Eden pulled himself from her. He wiped his eyes with the back of his hand.

"Does Dad know?" he said.

"He knows, darling. He thinks we need some time apart too." A thread cut. This is what upset me the most: that there was never a pull, a tug for us.

"How did you talk to him?" I said.

"Parvati let me use the telephone in her room."

"Didn't he ask about us?" Eden said, his voice sounding frantic.

"Yes, of course he did. I told him you had both made friends and looked so beautiful and healthy. . . ."

Her voice was slow, cautious, as though she were holding an envelope that she was afraid to open.

I imagined their conversation over the telephone. My mother standing in Parvati's rooms, our father in our house in London, hearing the phone ring.

He would stand up from the chair in front of the television, walk across the kitchen, reach for it.

"Hello?" he would say, and it would sound like *'Ello?*

"Simon? It's me, Lucy." My mother would say coldly, as she stood in Parvati's rooms, pressing the receiver to her ear, her heart beating quickly, a pounding in her throat. "I'm phoning to tell you that we're staying here in California. We're not coming back to London. I think it will be a better life for the children."

She would be standing still, not wavering, not flickering like the flame of the candle. Delivering the words Parvati had told her to say.

"A better life for the children?" he would repeat, knowing these were not her own words, a sentence she had not made up. His face turning, settling into one expression, listening to the dark tunnel down the telephone line. "All right, Lucy, if that's what you want. I don't have the energy to fight with you anymore. I'll be forty soon. A man my age wants to be settled. I don't want to grow old like this, fighting and breaking up all the time. I work hard and I want to have a nice life."

She would almost laugh. A nice life; like skates on ice. What a simple desire. This is why I'm leaving him! She'd stand victorious in Parvati's room, having left the world behind her. He would look at the things around him: the kitchen table and chairs, the stainless-steel sink, the long glass vase blooming with fresh flowers. He'd catch his reflection in the garden doors, standing alone in the kitchen of his house.

"Do you think he'll visit us here?" I asked her.

"Honestly, May, do you really think he's going to fly all this way for a visit?" She sighed, letting her arms fall against her sides.

I looked at her as she sat on the bed, holding her head in her hands. It was as though, at that moment, she had decided to let everything fall. I imagined paper grocery bags falling from her arms, the oranges rolling across the floor, the bottle of milk broken.

In the past she would have protected us from these things: the uncertainties, his casualness as a father. "Oh," she would say, covering her mouth with her hand, "I must have told him the wrong shoe size or the wrong time of your birthday party. Maybe I forgot to put the invitation in the post."

"I think he'll come here," Eden said, his voice like a balloon rising. "He'll surprise us and take us to Disneyland."

"Maybe he will, Eden," I said. I looked away from him, to the window, but it was dark outside and there was nothing to see. I knew our mother had told us the truth; our father would not come and visit us here. The flight would be too long, the tickets too expensive, and who would watch the shop while he was away?

When I was ten and Eden was four, my mother bought a house by the sea. It was her dream, she said, to live by the sea. She was going to turn the house into a small hotel, a bed-and-breakfast to pay the bills.

The first few weeks we were there, our mother telephoned her friends in London, telling them she had given up the city, given up the rat race. She talked quickly, loudly, into the telephone, explaining her reasons for leaving as though she were on trial. When she put the phone down, she stood by the window looking out to the sea, thinking of who she could call next.

We moved into the house in the late spring, and during the summer months her friends from London came to stay, but when the weather turned colder they didn't want to make the trip. The house was always cold, with cracks in the wood where a draft came through. The shutters banged in the wind at night, keeping everyone awake.

That first winter, we were alone at home and alone in the town. No one came to visit and it was difficult to make any new friends at school, where they had been together since they were six. Together, aimlessly, we walked up and down the main street and around the town, as a way to fill the end of the day.

Then we discovered a café on a side street. The café had small round tables and pale yellow walls. The warmth of baked bread and buns and vegetable soup steaming in tall pots.

The café became our favorite place. We went there after school and on the weekends, giving us a reason to leave the house. A reason to get out of our nightgowns, brush our hair, match our socks, and wash the dishes in the sink so everything would be tidy for our return.

The hot soups and cakes were the reward for a day of house-keeping: changing the bedsheets, washing, hanging the clothes to dry above the stove, waiting by the phone for someone to make a booking. A small hope, to fill an empty room.

In the café, our mother never said, We're losing money by the day. She never said, I've spent all the money I saved and this place is falling apart. The floorboards are rotting, the plaster is cracking, there's a hole in the roof. . . . She never said, I imagined another life in the country for us—a rabbit hutch, a garden, friends coming round, picnics in the fields. . . .

One evening in January, our father telephoned from London. He said he wanted to visit. He was taking a long weekend away from the shop to spend time with us.

When I put the phone down, I looked around the house anxiously. He would poke fun at the quaint bedrooms, some with matching curtains, bedspreads, and wallpaper.

In my bedroom, I examined myself in the mirror. I thought I needed a haircut, but then I noticed my stomach. In the cold weather, sitting around the house and eating pastries at the café, I had put on weight. Nowhere else really, just my stomach and waist, which rounded over the top of my trousers. My favorite jeans didn't button at the top anymore and they were skintight in the thighs, so they looked painted on.

That night, I did sit-ups on my bedroom floor. My forehead grew hot and prickly and afterward I couldn't sleep. When we drove to the café after school, I ordered a cup of hot water with a slice of lemon.

"Is that all you're having?" Mum asked.

"I'm on a diet."

"Oh, don't be stupid, darling."

I sipped my lemon and water. I tasted half a spoonful of soup. There was an ache in my stomach, as I watched Eden eating his éclair.

"Did one of the girls in your class say something to you?" my mother asked.

I shook my head. "All we do is come here," I said, "and my stomach's gotten fat."

"Everyone puts on a bit of weight in the winter," she said.

Eden licked the chocolate from his fingers. My mother spooned her soup. She looked away from me to the door, as though she were waiting for someone to arrive.

The week before our father came I did forty sit-ups a day and aerobics in front of the dresser mirror. I drank six glasses of water from the tap before each meal so I would feel full. As I lay in bed at night, too hungry to sleep, I could see the beginnings of a dip in my stomach and feel my hip bones through my skin.

The weekend he was meant to visit, there was an unexpected snowfall, a blizzard. In the humid air that blew off the sea, the falling snow around our house disappeared, leaving the ground a darker shade, as though it had just rained.

Our father telephoned from London; I could hear his voice coming through the receiver. He had not left London yet. He was listening to the news over the radio. The traffic was moving at a snail's pace and the snow was continuing to fall. He would have to make the trip another time. He didn't want to sit for hours on the roads in the snow.

My mother thought there was another reason why he didn't want to come. She thought he was afraid she would ask him for money. During the winter months, only a few people came to stay, and when they were gone the rooms sat still, so cold you could see your breath in them.

The last time she had asked him for money was over the telephone. She sat at the kitchen table in our small flat at the top of the bed-and-breakfast.

"How are you, Simon? Things at the shop all right?" Her voice falling like a slide. "You know I hate to ask you for money."

I heard his voice through the receiver. "Lucy, you have some bloody nerve. Why should I pay for children who don't live with me and I hardly ever see? You're the one who left. You took the children away."

I went to London to visit my father on the holidays, he paid me two pounds an hour under the table, plus lunch, to help him in the shop. I unpacked the parcels from India and Morocco. I dusted and polished the statues, cleaned the windows and counters, watched for thieves, and answered the telephone: "Good afternoon, you've reached Simon's."

The first time I did it, it was a quiet day and only a few customers had come into the shop. My father said he wanted to pop out for a bit; he had to stop by the post office and the bank, and then he was going to pick up some sandwiches for our lunch. He put his coat on, checked his pockets, and took an envelope from beneath the cash register.

"Toodle-loo, darling." He blew me a kiss from the door. The cold air from the street blew inside with a slight smell of petrol. The door closed behind him, and I watched through the window as he walked down the street, his scarf wrapped once around his neck.

Then he was gone and I was alone in the shop. I sat on a stool behind the cash register, looking toward the door at the people walking by, wondering if any of them would come in.

The walls were covered in brown-and-gold striped wallpaper, and the lights shone down warmly from the ceiling. Against the back wall lay an antique wooden daybed, covered with a quilt made of orange and purple silk. I touched the quilt with my hand; he had said not to sit on it. The bed was for decoration only.

The telephone rang and I took my hand from the quilt, look-ing in the direction of it.

"Hello? Simon's."

"Hello. May, is that you?"

I let out a breath. It was my mother's voice on the end of the line.

"Yeah, it's me, Mum."

Yesterday before I left she had gone to bed early, not feeling well. She had woken up when the bank manager phoned to tell her she was overdrawn and she sat at the table with a headache and cold. Eden had been asking for new trainers, the kind his friend had, an American brand, that cost twenty-five pounds.

"Hi, darling," she said. I pictured her sitting at the table in our house by the sea. "I'm just phoning to see how you are."

"I'm fine."

"How's your dad?"

"Fine."

When we said good-bye I put the phone down and stood look-ing down through the counter glass. Inside were antique statues and jewelry, the price tags turned down. If a customer asked to see one, the cabinet would have to be unlocked, the jewelry taken out, and the small tag studied under the light.

The key to the counter was kept behind a picture frame near the telephone. The key to the cash register was also hidden there.

I looked at the cash register. I thought, I should take some money and give it to my mother. I knew where I would hide the money: under the paper in my dresser drawer. Through the win-dow I watched people crossing the street. An old man sold newspa-pers on the corner.

I lifted the edge of the picture frame and took the key from behind it. I put the key in the register box and turned it, looking at the door. Inside were rows of twenties, tens, and fives and rolls of coins. I touched the corner of a twenty, but there were only a few and he would notice if one was gone. I pulled out a ten-pound note and quickly closed the drawer. I sat on the stool, waiting for my breath to settle. I still held the key from the register in my hand.

The door of the shop opened and the cool air rushed in from the street. My father stood looking at me, his face stiff from the cold.

"Everything all right while I was gone?"

"Yeah."

"Anyone come in?"

I shook my head. "No."

"Slow day." He untied his scarf and hung it on a coatrack. "Anyone phone?"

"Just Mum."

He unbuttoned his coat, turning away from me to hang it on the rack over his scarf. I had the key and the money in my hand. "What did she have to say?"

"She just wanted to say hi to me."

He looked at me from where he stood. "I got you a cheese and tomato sandwich. You like that, don't you?"

I nodded. "Thanks, Dad."

"Thanks, Dad," he said, mimicking me.

"And a delicious strawberry tart from the shop up the road." He turned the lock on the door and headed to the back of the shop where there was a mini kitchen behind the door. It was bad manners, he said, to eat at the register, in front of customers. It lowered the tone.

He opened the door. While his back was turned I slipped the money into my pocket and put the key behind the picture frame.

FOURTEEN

The ashram school began. The schoolhouse had not been built yet, so our classroom was the porch of Lotus House.

In the past, children on the ashram had gone to the public school in Rosemont, but there had been some incidents last year. A few of the students had used racial slurs toward Summer and her younger sister and brother. One of the boys in Summer's class had spat on her. His spit landed on her bare shoulder, and for the rest of the day she held her hand on that place, covering it like a scar.

Brad and Dylan had gotten in fights with a group of boys. One night, the ashram gates were toilet-papered and spray-painted. They wrote WELCOME TO FREAKY TOWN! DEVIL WORSHIPERS AND FAG-GOTS LIVE HERE.

After this, Parvati said the children would be taught on the ashram. A rectangle of ground had been broken behind the temple, and funds were being raised to build the school there.

In the mornings, Mum, Eden, and I ate breakfast together in the dining hall and then we walked to our classrooms. From the porch of Lotus House, I watched my mother and Eden walk to his classroom in the house across the pond. He wore the rucksack from his school in London. Mum kissed him good-bye at the door of the house and waited while he went inside with the other children. Afterward, she ran to the kitchen, where she would spend the day cooking for Parvati.

There were only four of us in my class: Sati, Summer, Molly, and me. We sat at a small table with Kelly at the head. I sat next to

Sati, and Summer and Molly sat across from us. I felt Sati touch my thigh under the table while Kelly handed out an article she had photocopied from a newspaper.

I reached down, touching Sati's fingers, and she pressed a small piece of paper into my hand. I glanced down, reading the note. *I'm so happy you are staying here.*

I smiled at Sati, crinkling the note in my hand.

Through the window, the sun fell in golden patches between the trees. In the frame of the window, the light and the trees looked more like a photograph than something real.

After school, Sati and I carried our books to the stables. We fed and brushed the horses and gave them clean water, and then we sat down on the bench to do our homework.

When we were finished with our homework, we climbed the ladder to the hay loft. She taught me things to do with my tongue that she had learned from her boyfriend in Denver. She taught me to give a blow job by sucking on her finger.

Sometimes we pretended to be other people. Sati was the handsome riding instructor and I was the student. I lay down on the floor and she was the doctor, examining me. Once, I found her near death at the foot of a tree from eating poisonous berries and I had to revive her with kisses. Sometimes, while we kissed, I pretended she was the boy at the dairy in Scotland, but this was a secret I never told her.

On the weekends we took walks through the grapefruit grove and sat by the river. When we were away from the stables, she took my hand in hers. Sometimes, a large golden dog who hung around the stable followed us.

Once he found a turtle crossing the path and carried it up in his mouth. "Drop that!" Sati yelled as she chased him, but he swerved between us and ran ahead, dropping it now and then to sniff and lick the turtle's shell, but when we were near him he picked up the turtle and ran away with his nose and tail high in the air.

The afternoon sun set behind the treetops, and mosquitoes and flies hovered around us. Sati swatted a mosquito on her arm "That's the only thing I'll ever kill," she said. We sat by the river, dangling our feet in the cool running water. The dog lay in the shade of a nearby tree. He had grown tired of the turtle and dropped it somewhere along the way.

When I looked at the stream disappearing through the trees, I thought of it as a road. I thought of Sati walking alone through the woods to the pay phone at the gas station and how I would be too afraid to walk there alone.

Our feet touched in the water.

"Sati?"

"Yeah."

"When did you start liking it here? I mean, when did you stop wanting to leave?"

Sati shrugged. "A couple years ago, I think."

"Why? What made you like it here?"

"I guess it was God."

"Oh."

Sati stared at the water, at the gray rocks beneath. Her hair fell straight around her face, and the sun reflected softly against her skin. I wondered what she was like when she first came here four years ago. What she was like as she walked by herself through the woods.

In Scotland, I used to dare myself to walk off the marked trail and into the woods. I was tempted to try to get lost. Tears came to my eyes when I thought of how much my mother would miss me when I was gone.

"She disappeared in the woods," the police would say. I imagined my father, his face turning gray when he heard the news. He would turn the lights out in the shop, lock the front door with shaking hands, and rush down the street. How much more would they love me when I was missing? I could feel the tightness, the embrace of being found.

In the woods I imagined that I would stumble upon an abandoned but furnished cottage, pick the berries that grew outside, and roast vegetables for dinner. There would be fresh clean water running by. None of this would take any effort; I would just know how to live in the woods.

I dared myself, stepping carelessly off the marked trail into the leaves and trees and sky, but after only a few steps I would panic and rush back to find the orange markers on the trees.

The school days were divided into hour-long classes of math, English, history, science, music, and art—the same as my school in London. There was one class we didn't have at my old school, it was called Current Affairs and Contemporary Issues.

We read an article called How Not to Be a Consumer. We watched a documentary about the Nestlé company selling baby formula in third-world countries. We saw an underground film that a friend of Kelly's from Brown had made, about animals in research laboratories, but we made her turn it off just before a scientist was about to drill a hole into a monkey's head.

Sometimes we had this class sitting in a semicircle on the porch. Kelly let us make orange juice smoothies from a tube of orange concentrate mixed with bananas and ice, so it came out thick and frothy. We drank the smoothies and ate rice cakes with almond butter and honey on top.

Our favorite subject in contemporary issues was Kelly's Sweet Sixteen party. There were one hundred guests at the party. They had a DJ and angel food cake with fresh strawberries and whipped cream. Kelly and her four best friends spent the day at a beauty parlor having their hair and makeup professionally done. Her boyfriend picked her up at her house with a corsage.

Molly and Summer, especially, loved to hear about Kelly's life in Beverly, Massachusetts. They asked her to bring in photographs of her house and family, to tell us about her summer vacations in Maine and the names of her childhood friends. Molly asked her to describe the bedroom she grew up in, and I could see, as she listened, that she was arranging the furniture in her head, like a dollhouse.

Molly was three and Summer was five when their parents came to the ashram, so they only had vague memories of their lives before. They could not remember living in their own house or having their own bedrooms. What was the school prom? What did Kelly's mother make for dinner every night? Did all girls have Sweet Sixteen parties? They chewed the erasers at the end of their pencils.

We all wanted to hear about Kelly's boyfriend Dave Mahony, the quarterback on the high school football team. But Molly and Summer's interest in Kelly's life, the way they sat knees to chest, reminded me of the nights in London I stayed up with Greta, listening to each word she used to describe her boyfriends. Sneaking a look inside her red suede purse while she put Eden to bed upstairs: a folded ten-pound note, Doublemint chewing gum, dark red lipstick, cigarettes, a pink plastic lighter, a black Filofax, and a purple polka-dot pen with purple ink. . . .

Before we left for California, Greta had stopped by the shop with some "exciting news." She had gotten a callback for a television commercial and her agent had phoned to tell her they thought she was really great, perfect for the role.

"It would run on all the stations," she said.

"All three?" Mum said, almost sarcastically.

I was still angry at Greta. Sometimes, I woke up furious in the middle of the night with a tight feeling in my throat.

Dear God—I mean, Dear Parvati—Please do not let Greta be on television. Can't they see how mean she is?

I would repeat this over and over, like a spell. And I believed, in a way, that I could cast a spell.

Then I was awake, thinking about Greta, and couldn't fall back to sleep. I lay in bed next to Eden and Mum, listening in the dark to the sound of their breathing.

Through the open window, the sound of the insects rose like a curtain around us. From where I lay, I could see the moon and my favorite star, the one closest to the moon.

It was already October, and the weather in England would be turning cold. Eden and I had only spoken to our father once since he left for India. He had telephoned from Delhi, and I stood in the kitchen, saying, "Hello. Can you hear me, Dad?" The connection was so bad all I heard was crackling and echoes down the line. Like the wallpaper in the linen closet, a surprise when you open the door, this was becoming the pattern of our lives.

In the dark, I counted on my fingers, trying to figure out what time it was in London and what would be happening there. At midnight, in California, the girls in my form would be waking up, dressing in their uniforms, eating bowls of cereal in their kitchens.

I imagined Samantha Fenton and Sheba Marks standing in the drizzle in the school courtyard, talking about my glamorous new life in California. I imagined the whole school was talking about me, the way I had imagined the audience was watching only me in the Christmas play.

I had never been cast as the lead in a school play, but even when I was one of the three angels, come to see the baby Jesus in the manger, I thought the spotlight was shining on me. I stood onstage in my white dress with gold wings, waiting, as though at the edge of a cliff, to deliver my one line: "I have come to bring you myrrh." The line that everyone would remember. They would say as they left their seats at the end of the play, "Who was the girl who played the part of angel number three?"

I hoped I was missed, but I knew I probably wasn't. Over the years a few girls in my form had left; some had moved away, others had gone to boarding school, but they were never missed for long. The memory of them faded over the summer holidays and was replaced by the excitement of the first day of school: new girls and returning girls, sitting at their desks, hanging their coats on their hooks, writing their names in their books.

My closest friend, Julia, left last year. She had won a scholarship to an academic all-girls public school in Ascot, where they wore brown tweed smocks in all types of weather. When I saw her on holidays she had dark circles beneath her eyes and little time to spend with me.

Before we left, I told her we were going away on holiday to California and would be back at the end of August. I wondered if she had telephoned or come knocking on our door.

I wondered as I lay awake at night, if our grandfather knew where we were. What had our mother told him? I tried to remember, but the words kept changing.

"We're going to America, for a holiday," she would have said.

"To visit your mother in New York?" he might have asked.

Anne, her beautiful mother, his ex-wife, who had left him years ago for a more exciting man.

What had she said? I couldn't remember now.

Did she say, "No, we are going to visit my friend Renee. She lives on an ashram."

"An ashram?" he would say, looking at his daughter in a peculiar way. "A guru? I've never heard of such nonsense."

She would not have told him; it would only have led to arguments over the phone. Still, we went away and we were his only family. We were a small family; leaving felt like breaking a plate.

An ashram was a place Grandfather would never understand. He wouldn't even try. He went to church occasionally. He respected the importance of religion in other people's lives, but he was not deeply interested in it. Psychiatrists and the very religious were kept in the same basket. Church was a place you visited at Christmas and at Easter, to hear the choir, gaze at the high ceiling, and greet old friends and village acquaintances, so they could see that you were still alive. Church was to be kept at a distance, like a handshake.

Mrs. Stirling believed in church. She believed that if you went to church at least three times a week, and not just for the coffee and cakes afterward, you would be granted a place in heaven when you were dead and buried.

God did not live on an ashram. God lived in church. The Church of Scotland, mainly.

I could hear her gossiping about us at the Sunday coffee hour.

"What has she done this time?" a friend would ask, as she stirred her tea with a concerned frown between her eyes.

"She's run off to an ashram in California with those two children and hasn't even telephoned her own father! Och, and after all he's done for her." Mrs. Stirling would shake her head in disbelief.

"Hasn't she always been a bit odd?" her friend would say.

"Just like her mother. The apple never falls far from the tree, I tell you. But it's such a shame. Bernard is a fine gentleman, and she's his only child."

"Is he worried about them?"

"Oh, he's not the type to complain. If my Julie ran off to an ashram I would be on the first flight, dragging her home by the scruff of her neck, but Mr. Bruce doesn't interfere. And to think, they haven't even telephoned! I wonder if they'll be home by Christmas?"

The concerned woman stirring her tea nods sympathetically. "Well, the poor girl, Lucy. I remember quite clearly when Anne left them. I saw Anne that day at the station, standing in her tweed coat and hat, a foxtail around her neck, wearing lipstick in a shade not suitable for a woman her age. I said, Where are you going, Anne? She said, I'm off to Harrods, to buy some sugared ginger for tea.

"With your luggage? I said to her. Well, she only nodded and looked away. Would never give me the time of day. I remember Anne even in our school days, prettier and thinner than the other girls; she always thought too much of herself. She stood so close to the platform edge, the toes of her shoes hung over, and I remember thinking, If there's a sudden gust it will blow her right over onto the tracks."

"Her death might have caused the two of them less pain," Mrs. Stirling said, then quickly crossed herself. Mrs. Stirling, a God-fearing woman with a shard of glass inside. "Well, I'll be in church most of next week," she said, "so I will pray for them all."

FIFTEEN

There was a game my mother and Caroline played. It was an old wives' tale my mother had learned from Nanny Hannah.

In the small house Sati's father had built, Caroline took off her wedding ring. My mother pulled out a strand of her hair and tied it to the ring. Sati and I sat on the floor watching them.

Caroline lay back on the sofa, her head propped up on a pillow, watching as my mother dangled the ring from a string over her belly. If the band circled clockwise, it was a girl. The other direction meant the baby was a boy. We sat without speaking as the gold band slowly began to turn at the end of the string.

Caroline sat up with excitement every time she felt the baby move inside her. She held my mother's hand in her hand, pressing it against her belly, so that she could feel the baby move too.

They stayed up late into the night, picking at leftover tea cakes and breads my mother would bring from Parvati's kitchen, talking about childbirth and babies. My mother suggested names, but with each name came a reason why it shouldn't be used: a mean girl in grade school, an alcoholic aunt. They sat up all night, throwing out names like cards.

While our mothers stayed up late talking in the dining hall, Sati and I would go back to her house. There was a game we liked to play too.

The first time it happened was by accident. We had come running out of the pond and fell on the path and were covered with sand, so we went back to her house to take a shower, but her mother was in the shower, so we ran a bath instead.

We sat across from each other at either end of the tub. The water was hot and full of bubbles. Sati told me to open my legs. I opened them slightly, but she put her hands on my knees, spreading them farther apart until they fell against the sides of the bathtub. She moved her hands down my thighs, to the center, and pressed the palm of her hand between my legs. She put her finger inside of me and rubbed her hand slowly up and down. I felt my eyes open wide. Then I closed my eyes and felt myself press against her; she moved her hands faster. I thought I would scream and held my mouth closed. The water was warm. My face grew hot as I pushed myself harder against her hands.

I felt a shudder, a pulsing. She kept her hand still between my legs, and when I opened my eyes, with a feeling of water running through me, she leaned forward, kissing me on the mouth, and told me to do it to her.

When I thought about this in class or in my bed at night, I could still feel the shudder of her hand between my legs.

On the weekend, I spent the nights at Sati's house. We slept together in the single loft bed at the top of the ladder. Before we fell asleep we tickled each other's backs and wrote words with our fingers, then erased them with the palm of our hands.

One night, Sati wrote the words *I love you.*

The game was usually relaxing, but I lay on the bed beside her, silent. She moved her hand beneath me, underneath my breasts, and kissed the back of my neck. She laid her mouth against my back, in the place were she had written the words. I didn't know what to say. I closed my eyes.

Her head lay against my shoulder. I wondered if she would hear my heart or notice how still I was. Why couldn't we have known each other in London? She could have lived next door. We could have met outside in the mornings in the damp air, and walked to school together, past the houses and shops, while the day brightened.

I opened my eyes. A skylight above the sleeping loft showed a square of the dark night and two stars.

"Sati?"

The weight of her head felt heavy against me.

"Mmm," she said, her eyes still closed. She rolled away, onto her side, her face hidden in the pillow and hair covering her eyes. How could she fall asleep on a night like this?

I touched her back and drew a line through the air from me to her. A line that would connect us, a line that would never break.

"I love you too," I said. I lay very still, almost frightened. This was the first time in my life I had said this to someone not in my family. The first time I had ever said these words to a friend.

SIXTEEN

In November, Caroline gave birth to a baby girl. Mum, Eden, and I went to visit her when she was just two days old. Our mother had baked a loaf of orange bread and made a vegetable quiche we carried to their house. Eden gave her a picture he drew of the solar system, and I picked her a bouquet of the wildflowers that grew near the grapefruit grove.

The baby had been born at the local hospital. It was an easy birth, Caroline said, her cheeks still flushed with excitement. She sat in a rocking chair, nursing, the baby's small head and soft dark hair against her chest, the baby's fingers curled in delicate fists.

"Have you thought of a name yet?" my mother asked.

"Parvati's going to name her," Sati said, looking up from where she sat beside her mother.

We stared at the baby in Caroline's arms. Sati touched the baby's head and John, Caroline's husband, offered us drinks. He opened the mini refrigerator in their house, kneeling down to take out a bottle of water and apple juice. He looked over at his wife.

"Honey, can I get you some more water?"

"No, thanks," Caroline said.

He brought the drinks to Eden, Mum, and me and then stood beside his wife, wrapping his arm over her shoulder and smiling at the baby.

"I'm older, but it was so much quicker this time!" Caroline said, amazed by it. "I was in labor for two and a half days with you," she said to Sati, "but you were worth every moment of it."

"Eden was nearly born in the backseat of the taxi. Simon was so stoned at the time, I couldn't get him up from the sofa. I kept saying, *I'm in labor,* and he said, 'Can't you wait till the advert?'"

Caroline burst out laughing.

"After May was born, the midwife in the hospital handed her to me and said, *From maiden to mother.* The first time I held her, it was as though my life suddenly came into focus and everything else just melted away."

"From maiden to mother." Caroline repeated the words, almost under her breath.

"Did I look like her when I was born?" Sati asked.

"You really did," Caroline said. "Look at the photograph by the window."

Sati walked to the window, taking a photograph in a silver frame from the sill. She touched the photo with her finger, clearing away the dust.

"Can I see, Sati?" I said, walking over to her.

In the photo, Sati lay in her mother's arm, wrapped in a pale yellow blanket.

"My grandmother knitted that blanket for me," she said. "I still have it, but it's thin, now, and the color's faded."

"Do your grandparents know about this baby?" I said, quietly so the others wouldn't hear.

Sati shook her head. She put the picture back on the windowsill, leaning it against the glass so it wouldn't fall.

Eden sat next to Mum; he reached out carefully, almost fearfully, to touch the baby. "You were like that, darling," she said, wrapping her arms around him. "Both of you. I remember it so clearly."

Sati leaned her head against her mother's shoulder. Here, in this room, with her mother and father, with her baby sister, she was like a young girl. In the moment of quiet we could hear the baby suckling, a soft purring sound.

John sliced pieces of orange cake and passed them out on plates. His quick, busy movements made him seem nervous. He refilled the pitcher of water next to Caroline's chair.

"I forgot how thirsty this makes you," she said, sipping from her glass.

John stood in the middle of the room with a camera. "Everyone say cheese," he said. Caroline set the glass of water down beside her and smiled.

John took the picture; there was a *click* sound and a flash. I imagined a frame around us, looking up at the camera, smiling.

Caroline picked up the drawing Eden had made for her. Eden sat up, his arms pressed close to his body, as she looked at the blue and white sky and the circling red and orange planets.

"Oh, look. It's so beautiful. You drew that by yourself?"

Eden nodded. He reached out to show her the different stars and planets.

"How did you learn so much about them?" she asked him.

Eden looked at Mum. "We studied them in school last year," he said.

"You draw them so beautifully," Caroline said.

"He's always drawn well," Mum said. "But he usually draws airplanes and army tanks."

The sun came through the windows, falling against the backs of our heads. The soft smell of the orange bread and the baby, the flowers on the table. I felt my mother beside me, the warmth of her shoulders against mine, and I remembered something she had said to our father once. Where were we? Were we driving in the car? Or was it in the kitchen of our house, where most things were said? Or had she written it in a note? A letter? The words were:

I hoped, when I became a mother, that I could give my children a happiness apart from daily life, apart from

the material things in the world—but how I planned
to do that, I don't know.

Caroline passed the drawing to Sati, and Sati passed it to her
father. Eden's cheeks blushed from the attention, and he sat up very
straight on the sofa. Mum ruffled his hair with her hand, her eyes
bright like his. Was this one of the moments our mother had spoken of, her children happy, peacefully sitting beside her, no one asking for anything, no one complaining? Would we see this moment
in the photograph John had taken, like a golden light around us?
How long could this feeling last? Would it leave when we left the
house? When we stood up to say good-bye? There was no reason to
leave this room, except for the hours passing and the end of the day.

That week in darshan, Parvati introduced the baby to the ashram.
She had chosen a name.

"My *chellas*," she said, "I want to introduce Jaya."

She held the baby up for the room to see.

The people applauded. Camera flashes went off and the baby
began to cry.

A voice in the room shouted, "Congratulations! You have a
beautiful daughter."

Caroline turned to the voice. "Thank you," she said, before
realizing the person was congratulating Parvati. Caroline sat next
to Parvati, waiting for her to hand the baby back to her. Parvati held
the baby in her arms, cooing loudly, tickling beneath her chin, but
it only made the baby cry more. Caroline reached out to take her,
but the reach of her arms was ignored.

Eden and I sat beside our mother. She was not cheering, clap-
ping with the others, or cooing at the baby. She had her arm around
Eden, her fingers pressed tightly against his skin.

Caroline watched. She had an anxious but helpless look in her eyes. I thought at any moment she would scream, *Give me my baby back, please?* John sat beside her, holding her hand in his. Sati sat beside Parvati's chair, staring up at her, enjoying the attention her sister was receiving.

In school, Sati told us about the baby. She loved being an older sister, she said. She took care of the baby when her mother needed to nap or take a shower; she changed her, bathed her, and sang her to sleep. As a special present, Sati gave Jaya the pale yellow blanket her grandmother had knitted for her when she was a baby.

When Jaya was one week old, Sati told us, her mother and Jaya moved out of their house and into Parvati's rooms. The baby's nursery was finally finished and Jaya could move in. Before the adoption, Caroline had suggested that she nurse the baby for the first few months, because it was the best thing for the baby, and Parvati had agreed.

"It's the prettiest nursery you've ever seen," Sati said. Summer, Molly, Kelly, and I sat on the porch, listening to her.

"I've never seen a nursery," Molly said.

"Maybe you had one when you were a baby," I said.

Molly shrugged. "I don't remember. What does it look like, Sati?"

"The walls are yellow, like pale lemon. Renee painted the ceiling with stars and a crescent moon. She painted bunny rabbits and flowers and grass around the bottom of the walls. Jaya has a white crib with a lace canopy and shelves and shelves of toys. Parvati's devotees sent them from all over the world. She's too young for them now, but soon she'll play with them. Parvati said in a month or two, when Jaya's older, I can take you all to see her in the nursery."

"That would be exciting," Kelly said. "The only part of Parvati's house I've been in is the main room and the gardens."

"Does Jaya cry a lot?" Summer asked.

Sati shook her head. "She mostly just eats and falls asleep in my mom's arms. Yesterday the Women brought in an extra bed for me, because Parvati said I could sleep there on weekend nights."

I looked at Sati, but she did not notice me. Her eyes slid over us, eager to tell us more.

"Oh, and Keshi and Lucy bring our food on a tray and make us whatever we want from the kitchen."

"Wow," Kelly said, but her voice was uncertain. "It sounds like a hotel, with room service and everything."

"How long is your mother going to stay with her in the nursery?" Summer asked.

Sati shrugged. "A couple weeks or something. A month? I'm not really sure."

"Then she's going to have to leave?" I said.

Sati nodded.

"Who will take care of the baby after?" Molly asked.

"Parvati will," Sati said, but there was a nervousness in her voice as she answered our questions.

"Okay, girls," Kelly said, looking at her wristwatch. "Our break ended ten minutes ago, so let's get back to the classroom."

This was the first time that a disciple of Parvati's had given her their child, and even Molly and Summer, the girls who had lived longest at the ashram, listened to Sati's tales with a slight unease.

Now that Parvati had a baby daughter, she wanted other babies to be born on the ashram, so that Jaya would have playmates and friends.

In darshan, Parvati announced that she had had a message from her guru that Amba and Old Durga Das were to marry and have a child.

Amba's face turned ashen when Parvati announced that she would be old Durga Das's bride. Amba lived in the room next to ours with a roommate. That night we could hear her sobbing through the walls while her roommate tried to comfort her.

There was no way she could have sex with Old Durga Das. He repulsed her. She would not be able to love a baby of his. She contemplated telling Parvati that she wanted to become a monk and take a vow of celibacy.

Amba was in her early thirties. She was short with curly red hair and freckles. She was a dancer and taught dance to us twice a week at school. She dressed in leotards and leg warmers and practiced her dance moves and stretches in the living room downstairs. Sati and I liked to talk about her chest, because she was flat as a boy.

Old Durga Das, the man she was supposed to marry, was almost sixty-two. He had thin legs, like sticks, and a potbelly. He wore trousers with suspenders and occasionally a bow tie. Before he moved here, he had been a professor at a state college in Florida and had a habit of pointing his finger at you when he spoke. What I remember most clearly, though, were his hands. One night, as I stood beside him in line for dinner, I saw that even though he was a tall man, his hands and fingers were as small as a young boy's.

Amba and Old Durga Das were married by Parvati in a ceremony outside the temple. My mother and Keshi baked the wedding cake, a large lavender-frosted cake in a flat pan decorated with fresh flowers and silver cake balls.

Amba wore a long flowered dress and a wreath of wildflowers in her hair. She clutched her bouquet tightly in her hands, with seven bridesmaids trailing her. She smiled so widely, as she walked toward the altar, you could see all her teeth. The closer she came to the temple, where Old Durga Das stood in his badly fitting suit and black bow tie, you could see that through her smile her face was covered in tears. If I hadn't known that she did not want to marry him, I would have thought she was crying for joy. I would have thought she was the happiest bride I had ever seen.

SEVENTEEN

Sati took me to visit her sister in the nursery. In the room, Caroline sat in a rocking chair with the baby on her lap. I could hear her singing softly while the baby slept. I looked around at the pale yellow walls and up at the ceiling with its pattern of moons and stars.

"Hi," Caroline said quietly, when she saw us. In the corner stood a white crib with matching pale yellow sheets and a colorful mobile hanging above. She put her finger to her lips, whispering that the baby had just fallen asleep.

Sati and I sat down on a single bed covered in a dark blue bedspread with silver mirrored pieces in the trim. My father had sold these bedspreads at the shop. A small suitcase lay on the floor; a glass of water and a bottle of rose-scented hand lotion sat by the lamp on the bedside table.

Rose lotion and a book; there was nothing else of Caroline's in the room.

A smaller bed, the size of a hotel cot, sat across the room.

"Is that your bed, Sati?" I asked.

"Yeah. It's just temporary. Parvati told me she was going to make me my own room one day."

"Did she?" Caroline asked. "So you could be near your sister?"

The curtains were pulled closed, the dull light reminded me of nap time when I was a child.

Since Caroline had moved into Parvati's room, my mother had hardly seen her, and I knew she missed her friendship. At night she would walk into the dining hall alone, standing in the room holding her tray of food looking around for someone to sit with. Usually, she would find an empty place at the long communal table in the back. Sometimes she sat with Renee, but the two of them did not laugh together or stay talking late into the night over tea and dessert, the way she and Caroline had.

Caroline lifted the sleeping baby from her lap and walked with her to the curtained window, where the pale yellow light fell over them. "I'm going to try to rest for a while," she said. "I have not been sleeping well. Even when she's asleep, I can't sleep. I keep thinking I only have a few more weeks with her, and I don't know how I'll be able to leave her now."

"You knew you were only going to stay here for a little while, Mom," Sati said.

Caroline nodded. "I know I did, Sati." She walked away from the window to the bed. "I should have never looked at her or held her, because now that I have I never want to leave."

She lay down under the covers with the baby cradled in her arms. "I have to try to sleep now," she said again.

Caroline lay on the bed, her head touching the baby's, and closed her eyes.

Sati stood beside them. She pulled the bedspread over her mother's shoulders, tucking it below her chin. She leaned over and kissed her mother and the baby good night.

After school each day, Sati rushed to the stables and through chores, then ran to see her mother and sister in the nursery. She often left the stables early, leaving me to put away the buckets, secure the feed, and make sure the horses were fine for the night. On the weekends she would spend most of the day in the nursery, and she always spent the nights there.

I missed our weekends together, taking walks through the grapefruit grove and having sleepovers at her house. I thought, It's just new and soon she'll grow tired of the baby and of spending so much time in Parvati's rooms. There was nothing to do in the nursery really; all Jaya did was sleep and eat. I thought of the pale yellow light through the curtains and how it gave the room a warm and sickly feeling.

I knew Caroline would have to leave the nursery soon, and I looked forward to that day. I couldn't wait until Sati and I would have more time to spend after chores in the hay loft, and on the weekends when I would spend the night at her house again. We would eat dinner together in the dining hall and go to her house when no one was there and run a bath.

In our room at night, I told Eden to write a word on my back, and when I closed my eyes I would pretend it was Sati. But he would giggle and write the word *bum* or *fart* and I would swat his hand away.

I would lie in bed and think of exciting things I could tell her in school the next day, or I would look in the mirror, trying on things to wear or doing something new with my hair, to get her to notice me again.

There was a bathtub in the bathroom of our house. In the middle of the day, or sometimes on a Sunday, when the house was quiet, I would lock the bathroom door and run a bath. I sat in the warm water and with my own hands I pushed my knees apart. I would imagine they were Sati's hands; that she was saying, "Open your legs, open them wider." I ran my hands down my thighs and pressed my palms against myself, putting one finger inside. I moved my hand up and down. I imagined it was her and felt myself grow warm, thinking of Sati with my eyes squeezed tight.

EIGHTEEN

The weather in California grew colder. The skies were still blue in the daytime, but the sun lost its glare and heat.

In the dining hall one night, Molly and Summer and Brad and Dylan told Eden, Jabe, and me what Christmas used to be like on the ashram. A devotee of Parvati's from Los Angeles worked for the toy company Mattel, and at Christmastime a truckload of brand-new toys would arrive. There were board games, roller skates, Barbie dolls and Dream Houses, toy cars, new bikes with banana seats and streamers—all brand new and still smelling of plastic from the factory. But in the past couple of years, the toys were donated to local hospitals instead. It was the end of December, and Christmas had gone by unmentioned.

In London, the weather would be cold and damp. On our street, the Christmas lights on the trees would sparkle through the windows of the houses. I thought of our father, boiling water at the stove for his morning coffee and drinking at the table by himself.

I wondered where he had spent Christmas day. He had probably slept late, read the paper, then gone round to his friend Rafael's flat in Notting Hill, where the walls were papered in newsprint.

* * *

I thought of Grandfather walking through his house, turning off the radiators and shutting doors, closing rooms to save the heat, rooms with beds that lay covered in white sheets that would not be seen again until the spring.

I wondered where he had gone for Christmas day. We usually spent Christmas with him and bought a tree from the farmer and put it up by the fire. Maybe he had spent the day alone, waiting for it to pass. He was a reserved man, without many friends.

The fields around his house would be turning pale. The grass would be frozen white at dawn, shining with ice.

The Scottish sky turned dark by three.

The long hours inside the houses.

In between the pages of a book our mother had brought with her to read on the airplane, Eden and I found a paper menu from the carry-out restaurant down the road from our house in London.

In our room at night, we read the menu aloud to each other.

"What would you choose," Eden asked me as we lay on the bed, "if you could have just one thing?" He read from the list:

Shepherd's pie
Tweed kettle pie
Welsh rarebit
Bangers, mash, and beans
Fish and chips

I couldn't decide what to order, Welsh rarebit or fish and chips with lots of vinegar. I imagined the steaming plates of hot food and the plastic red-and-white checkered tablecloths. The crowd of people at lunchtime, on a workday, in the café. Umbrellas by the door, still wet with the rain.

"Fish and chips," I said suddenly, taking the menu from him. "Okay, Eden, what would you choose? You can only pick one."

He closed his eyes tightly as I read from the list of puddings. I felt an ache in my stomach, thinking about them.

Apple crumble
Warm spicy ginger cake
Trifle
Treacle pudding
Sticky toffee pudding
—all puddings served with hot custard

"Oh, no," he moaned, holding his hands over his stomach. "I want them all."

"Well, you can only choose one."

"Treacle and custard," he said. "No, wait!" He pressed his hand to his forehead as though agonized by his decision. "Or sticky toffee pudding. . . . *Please* can I choose both?"

I shook my head. "Just one."

This became our favorite thing to do when we were alone in our room at night. Soon the menu grew thin and worn from being held so often. The restaurant down the road was the place where we would all go at least twice or three times a week. When I read the menu I imagined us there, but that time was gone now and someone else was sitting at our table.

We were doing homework and reading the take-out menu when our mother walked into the room. It was early for her to be back from the kitchen, where she usually worked until ten or eleven. She stood in the doorway, slightly out of breath, and closed the door behind her. She stood, looking at us and the room, with her back to the door.

"What's the matter, Mum?" I looked up from my book.

She shook her head. "Parvati has asked me to look after Jaya in the nursery."

"She has?" I said, surprised at the excitement in my voice.

Everyone knew Parvati was looking for people to take care of her daughter; it was considered an honor.

"She wanted someone who had experience with babies, that's why she asked me." Mum sat down on the edge of the bed and she pressed her palms to her eyes. "She asked Keshi and Lotus too. I'm doing the evening shift."

"So you won't be working in the kitchen anymore?"

She shook her head.

"Do you have to sleep there, Mum?" Eden said. He came and sat beside her and she held him close, pressing him tightly to her, as though she were afraid of him being taken away.

"Some of the night. I don't know if I should do this."

"I thought everyone wanted to look after Jaya," I said.

"They think it's a way to be closer to Parvati," she said. "I saw Caroline this afternoon, and she looked terrible. John said she has hardly slept or eaten anything since she had to leave the nursery."

"Well, Caroline knew this was going to happen eventually," I said.

My mother sighed, looking at me. "You sound like Sati."

I touched a line in my book with the tip of my finger, as though I could stop this moment.

"How long are you going to stay in the nursery for?" Eden asked.

"I don't know, darling." Our mother turned, looking at the clock on the shelf, and stood up, straightening her skirt. "I have to go," she said quickly.

She walked over to the closet and pulled her carry-on bag from the shelf. She packed her nightshirt and took her toothbrush from the cup. She packed a sweater and took her small traveling pillow from the bed.

"I'll be back in the early morning; maybe I'll get some sleep then," she said. "Eden, please brush your teeth and wash your face before bed. Will you make sure he brushes his teeth properly, May?"

I nodded.

"Mum," Eden said. "I don't want you to go."

She looked at him, and I thought she would cry.

"You'll be with May," she said, touching the side of his face. "And if you need anything, I'll be in Parvati's house. I'll ask the Women to get me, for any reason. Okay, darling?"

She kissed us good-bye. She put her bag over her shoulder and let herself out of the room, closing the door behind her.

When she was gone, Eden sat without moving, looking toward the door.

On the weekend, Eden and I were allowed to visit our mother in the nursery. Sati said she wanted to come with us, so we left the dining hall after breakfast and walked together to Parvati's house.

We could hear the baby crying as we walked down the hallway to the nursery room. Inside, our mother walked the baby around the room, trying to calm her.

"She's been crying like this for hours, and she won't take anything from the bottle. I've had to spoon-feed her, and she spits most of it up."

"I'm sure she'll eat when she gets hungry enough," Sati said.

My mother gave her an impatient look. "Babies can get dehydrated very easily, and clearly she's miserable." She turned away from Sati with the crying baby in her arms, stopping herself from saying something more.

I looked away from them, to the window. Outside it was a cool day, but the sun shone brightly inside Parvati's garden. From the window, I could see the swimming pool and the rows of flowers planted along the stone path.

Eden walked around the room looking at the baby things and touching them: the wooden train set, the stuffed animals on the shelf. Above the crib he spun the colorful mobile.

"Look at that." He turned it again, so it twisted on its string. "Mum, did I have a mobile when I was a baby?"

"Yes, you did. Sati," my mother said, "why don't you try to comfort her?"

Sati held her arms out to take her sister and my mother carefully passed her the baby, holding her hand beneath the baby's neck. When her arms were empty, she let them drop heavily to her sides, relieved not to be holding her anymore.

"Jaya, shush," Sati whispered to her as she walked. "Why are you crying?"

My mother sat down on the bed watching her. She had been up for the last two nights, she said, with the crying baby. Her shoulders fell forward and her back hunched as she rested her head in her hands.

"Sati," our mother said. "How is your mother doing?"

"I think she's feeling better. My father took her to the doctor and he prescribed some pills."

In the past few weeks, I had only seen Caroline a few times. I saw her walking hand in hand with her husband around the pond, slowly, like an elderly couple. I had seen her in the dining room, sitting with Sati and John, touching the food on her plate with a fork.

Sati held a stuffed duck to Jaya's nose. "Quack, quack!" she said, and for a moment Jaya stopped crying, looking at the duck in amazement.

My mother picked the bottle up from the bedside table and took it over to Sati. "Maybe you should try to feed her."

Sati sat down in the rocking chair with the baby on her lap. She touched the rubber nipple of the bottle to her lips, but the baby turned her head away.

"I'm sure she'll get used to the bottle eventually," Sati said. She held her sister's tiny hand, telling her she would come back soon. "May and I have to go to chores now, but I'll come and see you soon," she said, as she kissed the back of her hand. The baby's eyes followed Sati, and when she saw that she was walking away, she began to cry again.

Sati and I walked to the stables. The weather was cooler now; there had been an overnight frost that turned the grass the color of straw.

"Poor horses," I said. "The grass is all dry and pale."

"There hasn't been enough rain this year," Sati said.

"There's always enough rain in England."

"There may be rain, but there isn't enough sun and everyone knows that the sun is more important than the rain." Sati said as she stared out at the horses in the field.

I saw Eden and Jabe running past us in a group of boys.

"What are you doing?"

Eden turned, looking back at me as he ran. "We're going to our fort!" His voice trailed behind him in the air. In the months we had been here, he had grown taller and thinner. He had outgrown the clothes he came with and now his shirts were too short in the arms and stomach. His tan skin gave him a sinewy, taut look he had not had before.

Inside, I filled the buckets with fresh water while Sati spread clean hay on the floor. I watched her as she went out in the field to brush the horses. Now that her mother had moved out of the nursery, I knew Sati would not be spending the night there, so when we were finished with the chores, she would not rush away. There was a small broken mirror over the sink and I looked at myself, combing my hair to the side with my fingers. Maybe today we would walk to the grapefruit grove together and sit by the stream.

I took another brush down from the shelf and walked out to the pasture.

"Sati," I said. "When we're finished do you want to go for a walk in the grapefruit grove?"

"It's a little cold today," she said, as she continued to brush the horse's mane.

The sky was gray and white with clouds, and a breeze blew in from the direction of the woods.

"Maybe it will rain," I said.

"Maybe."

"Do you miss staying in the nursery with your sister?" I asked. My voice sounded unsure, wavering.

"Maybe, a little bit. But Parvati said she would turn one of the extra rooms into a room for me. When Jaya's a little older, she said I would be allowed to take care of her."

"I took care of Eden when he was a baby," I said.

"By yourself?" Sati asked, turning to me.

I shook my head. "No, my mother was there."

"That's not the same," she said.

The other night, when we were alone in our room, my mother had said she didn't know how Caroline could go through with giving her baby to Parvati. It would be even harder, now that she had held her and nursed her and slept in the bed with her.

I remembered walking home from the hospital after Eden was born and the way Mum held him so carefully, so close to her. Looking over her shoulder, fearful of every passing car, of a group of schoolchildren running down the street.

At home we sat with him on the sofa, watching him sleep while Hannah brought my mother cups of tea and cooked soups and stews in the kitchen.

"I feel sorry for her," I said.

"Who?"

"Both of them, I guess, but Jaya misses her mother and she won't understand why she left or where she's gone." I remembered the way Eden had cried and Mum was the only person who could comfort him.

"Jaya's the luckiest baby in the world," Sati said. "Everyone wishes Parvati was their mother."

I looked away from her, touching the bristles on the brush with my fingers. "I don't."

Sati turned to me. There was an expression in her eyes, a squint, as though she were looking at me from far away. I knew I had said the wrong thing, the one thing that would chip away at our friendship.

I stared down at the pale grass, kicking it with my toes. I felt a stinging in my eyes and wondered if Sati could see I was fighting back tears.

We stood out in the horse pasture without speaking. The horses slowly walked away, eating the grass, their bodies moving past us.

Sati rubbed her arms with her hands. "It's getting cold."

"Yeah," I said.

I looked up at the sky; the clouds were still, not white and not gray. I held out my hand, but there was no rain.

"Do you want to go to dinner?"

"I think I'm just going to go home. I'm not very hungry," Sati said.

We carried the brushes back to the stables and put them on the shelf. We turned off the light and closed the gates.

"We have a quiz in math tomorrow," Sati said.

"I know. Have you studied for it yet?"

Sati shook her head. "Have you?"

"No."

The wind blew stronger. As we walked across the field, I crossed my fingers. This feeling, like a tightrope between us will end soon, I thought. It will be gone by the time we reach the path.

NINETEEN

In class, Kelly passed out photocopied sheets of paper called the ERBs. Kelly said she didn't approve or believe in standardized tests, but we had to study for them anyway. It had to do with being a legal school in the state of California and the "success" of the students.

Whenever the word "success" was used on the ashram it was said with quotation marks around it. Kelly thought the tests were classist and racist. "For example," she said, as she looked over the list of vocabulary words. "Cutlery. If you aren't living in a middle- or upper-class home, when would you ever hear this word used?"

I had never heard the word cutlery used in my house, but I nodded in agreement with Sati, Summer, and Molly, as we looked up at her from around the table.

In the afternoon, there was a knock on the classroom door. It was Keshi.

"Hello, girls," Keshi said. She was dressed festively, in a short floral skirt and a white blouse with a string of Rudraksha beads around her neck. She had tucked flowers into the bun on top of her head, so that it looked like a small hat.

"I have an announcement to make today," she said excitedly.

Sati, Summer, Molly, and I looked up at her. Kelly sat beside us; from the knowing smile on her face, it was clear that she knew what Keshi was going to say.

"As most of you know, or maybe some of the newer ones do not yet know"—Keshi stopped to smile—"once a year, Parvati has a slumber party for all the children."

I felt Sati squeeze my arm. She jumped up excitedly.

"So," Keshi said, holding her hands together, "tonight is kids' night with Parvati! Chores are canceled! Go back to your rooms and bring your sleeping bags and pajamas and meet outside Parvati's rooms at—" Before she could finish, Summer, Molly, and Sati were jumping up and down screaming with excitement.

"Calm down, please." Keshi said, pressing the air with her palms.

"Girls, girls!" Kelly said, stepping in. "I understand how excited you are, but before we leave for the day we have to quiet down and put our papers and books away."

Summer, Molly, Sati, and I stood talking outside about what to wear to Parvati's that evening.

"I'm going to wear my red denim skirt," Summer said.

"Do we have to dress up?" I asked.

"We have to look nice, like we do for darshan."

"Oh." I was thinking of what to wear. The few nice things I had were dirty.

"You can borrow something of mine if you want," Sati said. "My dad brought me back some new jeans when he went to Denver."

"Thanks," I said, looking at her. It was a clear day and the sunlight shone down, as though it were shining through glass.

Sati and I walked to her house. As we walked across the deck we could see her mother and my mother, through the screen door. They were sitting next to each other on the sofa, talking quietly.

*   *   *

Sati opened the door and her mother looked up at her, her hand on her chest, as though she'd been frightened.

"Sati?" her mother held the baby, Jaya, in her arms. Her shirt was unbuttoned, as though she had just been nursing her. The baby lay quietly in her arms, asleep, her head flung back in relief.

"Mom, what are you doing?"

My mother sat beside her; she looked away, clasping her hands together.

"Sati," her mother began to say calmly, "Jaya wouldn't eat. She's been crying for the last few days. I had to feed her."

"But Parvati said you weren't allowed to."

My mother glanced at Sati. "I think your mother knows what's best for the baby."

Sati stood quietly, watching them. I stood next to her, biting my fingernail.

"Maybe I should take her back now," my mother said to Caroline.

Caroline stared down at the baby in her arms. "Why are you girls home from school so early?" she asked.

"It's kids' night with Parvati," Sati said.

"What's kids' night with Parvati?" my mother asked.

"We have a sleepover and watch movies," I told her.

"Is Eden going?"

"All the children are invited," Sati said.

Caroline handed the baby to my mother. She buttoned her blouse before following her to the door. My mother placed the baby in a sling she wore around her shoulders. The sling was hidden beneath a shawl she fastened at the neck. I knew now that she had taken the baby from the nursery in secret and brought her here.

*   *   *

Caroline came back into the house; we heard the door fall shut behind her. She went to the sink and poured herself a glass of water.

"Are you girls thirsty or hungry?"

"No, Mom," Sati said. She knelt on the ground, unzipping a suitcase that still had the tin smell of airplane air around it. She pulled out two pairs of brand-new Sasson jeans with the tags pinned to the pockets. Beneath the jeans were four new blouses; all the same style and size, but each a different color. "Try these on," Sati said to me. She held one of the new pairs of jeans up to my waist. They were dark blue, cardboard-stiff, and I knew they would be tight on me.

We dressed in front of the mirror. She said I could wear one of her new blouses too, the mustard-yellow one. Sati wore the turquoise-blue one and a pair of earrings her mother loaned her. Her jeans did up easily around her waist but I had to lie down, sucking in my stomach. When I stood up, a layer of flesh hung around my waist. I untucked the blouse, holding in my stomach.

"That looks good, but you have to unbutton the top buttons of that blouse." She stood in front of me, undoing the buttons.

"Don't you think that's too low?" I asked, looking in the floor-length mirror. The skin of my chest showed beneath the collar.

"No." Sati shook her head.

"Yours is buttoned."

"We can't dress exactly the same. You can wear your own clothes, if you want."

She put her arm around me, looking at us both in the mirror. "We look better than the dancers on *Solid Gold*," Sati said, tilting her head to the side and posing with her hand on her hip. I smiled, copying her pose, tilting my head toward hers.

Outside, Sati realized we had left the sleeping bags behind, so we went back to get them. Inside the house, Sati's mother was sitting on the sofa, where she had sat with the baby. She held her hands to her face and cried.

"Mom?" Sati said, from the door. "Mom, are you all right?"

Her mother could not answer, she cried recklessly, like a child, trying to catch her breath between sobs. Sati sat down beside her. I stood for a moment just inside the door, unsure of what to do. Sati put her arm around her mother's back and stroked her hair with her hand. "It's all right, Mom," she said softly. Sati held her mother; she kissed the side of her face.

I picked up the sleeping bags from the floor and opened the door quietly to wait outside. When my mother cried, I was never able to soothe her like this. The way Sati comforted her mother, it was as though she were the mother and her mother was the child.

I stood outside the house, in Sati's tight jeans and yellow blouse, unbuttoned too low. The early evening was growing cool and the shadows of the trees slanted like bars across the path. Two men and a woman walked by. The woman was skipping, dressed in a red skirt. The color flashed through the trees.

I held my sleeping bag tightly as Sati and I walked along the path to Parvati's house. I looked at Sati; had she been crying too? But her profile as we walked was plain, her eyes dull from the light, her straight hair falling to the middle of her back, the small slope of her nose, her lips slightly parted, the evening light falling flat against her. I had never seen Sati cry.

TWENTY

The waiting area outside of Parvati's rooms was crowded with all the children on the ashram and their sleeping bags, pillows, and overnight bags. The younger children, like Eden and Jabe, had been pushed to the back, where they sat on the floor playing a game of jacks. Summer and Molly played a game of cards with Brad and Dylan in front of the doorway.

Soon the door opened and Keshi and Renee walked out. "It's time for kids' night with Parvati to begin!"

Everyone cheered, and there was a rush to the door.

"Whoa!" Renee said, holding her hands out in front of her. "Take it easy, now." I had never heard the word *Whoa!* used in England, but here the adults said it all the time: when we were about to step on the newly washed floors or cut the dinner line to get the warm oatmeal-honey cookies before they were gone.

Everyone was talking loudly, excitedly, in Parvati's room, waiting for her to arrive. There was a girl sitting by the side of Parvati's chair, in the spot that Sati usually sat in. Her name was Valerie. She was in the grade below us at school. She had moved here a few weeks ago from Texas with her mother and younger sister.

When Valerie saw Sati, she moved over, without being asked, so that Sati could have her regular spot, closest to Parvati. Valerie turned to Sati, looking at her with a hopeful smile.

When we were settled, Parvati came into the room, followed by Renee and Keshi. Keshi and Renee stood beside her as some of the children reached out for hugs and kisses. She announced that they had ordered pizza and ice cream. Parvati put her finger to her lips. "Don't tell your parents," she said. "They'll be so jealous."

The pizza arrived and we ate it on paper plates. It was still hot, the cheese sliding off as we lifted the slices from the box. Parvati and the Women ate pizza too.

Renee carried the ice cream cake into the room. "Oh, yeah, Zamboni! Zamboni!" Dylan sang, as he played air guitar.

Parvati and the Women laughed.

The ice cream was cut from a long cake of strawberry, chocolate, and vanilla stripes. Keshi cut us all equal-size pieces and served them on paper plates. I watched Eden, as he held the paper plate of ice cream in two hands, walking carefully back to where Jabe and the other boys were sitting.

While we ate the ice cream, Parvati told us to gather around her. We sat on the floor, on the plush red carpet in her receiving room. The glass doors looked out to the gardens and the lighted swimming pool shone in the night.

"My *chelas*," she said, "you are my children; you know that, don't you?"

"Yes, Parvati," we said in chorus. "Everything we talk about in here is a secret. You can tell us whatever you like."

Molly was the first to raise her hand. She told Parvati that she had had an argument with her mother. She had called her mother fat, which she knew was wrong, but her mother slapped her across the face.

"She hit you?" Parvati said, sounding astonished. She looked to Keshi and then Renee. "I will talk to her, Molly. And don't worry, she will not be mad at you."

"Parvati," Brad said, standing up with his nunchaku in his hand. "I was wondering if I could do a demonstration, because when I'm eighteen I would like to guard the gates."

"With those?" Parvati asked. "We'll lose our heads. All right, stand over there. Over there, way far away, in the back of the room."

We watched as Brad swung the sticks around in the air, karate-kicking and punching at imaginary intruders.

"Haven't I taught you nonviolence?" she asked. "Sit down. I'll think about it when you're eighteen."

Brad sat down, red-faced and out of breath.

The new girl, Valerie, raised her hand. "Parvati," she said. Her voice had a sleepy sound. "I just wanted to tell you I am so happy to be here."

Parvati smiled lightly at the girl.

"When we lived in Texas, my mother and her boyfriend had terrible fights. They were so loud they would wake me and my sister up. One night," Valerie continued, "I was making dinner for my sister when the toaster oven caught fire. The fire alarm went off and we were alone in the house. I tried to reach the telephone, but it was too close to the fire. I put the fire out with cups of water from the sink, but I had ruined the new toaster and the kitchen curtains."

"You must have been very frightened," Parvati said to her.

Valerie nodded. "When my mom's boyfriend came home, he hit me and called me names for ruining his new toaster. He said I had to save up to buy him a new one."

"He's not here. He will never be here," Parvati said to her.

Valerie began to cry.

"Come here," Parvati held her tightly. "I promise you," Parvati said, "you will never be frightened like that again. Not while you are here with me."

I noticed Sati watching Valerie while Parvati spoke to her. When Valerie had wiped her tears, Parvati put a string of Rudraksha beads around her neck.

"Is there anyone else?" Parvati asked, but no one responded. She looked over the room. Then Sati raised her hand.

"My Sati?"

Sati hesitated; she held her hands together in her lap. "I know someone who's broken a rule."

"Who?"

"Lucy took Jaya out of the nursery. She took her to see my mother in our house, and my mother nursed her."

I saw Renee turn to Keshi.

"Lucy took Jaya out of the nursery?"

"Yes."

"Did you see them?"

"Yes."

"When?"

"I saw them this afternoon. May was with me; she saw them too," Sati said.

I pressed my hands against the carpet when Parvati looked at me, waiting. "She had to," I said. "The baby wouldn't eat, and she was worried about her."

Parvati nodded. "I see."

"Thank you for telling me, my *chellas*." Parvati beckoned us to come to her, and held us in her arms together. Parvati whispered to Keshi, and Keshi handed her two necklaces; a single Rudraksha bead on a red string. Parvati put one necklace over my head and one over Sati's head. "You are very brave girls for telling me this."

Peter Runyun sat beside Parvati and played songs on his guitar, and we sang along. Sati sat next to me; she held the single bead on her necklace as she swayed back and forth to the songs.

After the singing, Parvati went back to her private rooms and Renee offered us a choice of movies to watch: a romance or a horror movie about children who are turned into vampires. There were mostly boys in the room, and they voted for the horror movie. During the movie, Keshi brought us bottles of seltzer water and big bowls of popcorn to share.

We sat down on the floor with our pillows and sleeping bags, watching the movie and eating popcorn. In the movie, regular children were turned into vampires by their friends while they slept in their beds. The most frightening scene in the movie was when a vampire boy floated up to the window of his friend's bedroom, scratching on the glass to get inside. I thought, Now, whenever I see a window at night, I'll think of this.

When the movie ended, most of the younger children had fallen asleep on their sleeping bags. In the blue light, I saw Eden sleeping on his stomach, his blanket covering his legs, his hands tucked beneath his pillow.

Dylan, Brad, Summer, Molly, Sati, Valerie, and I were still awake, eating the last of the popcorn. Brad jumped on Dylan, pretending to bite his neck and turn him into a vampire.

"Hey, guys," Brad said. "Let's go outside."

"Won't they hear us?" Molly asked.

"No. The bedrooms are on the other side," Brad said. He knew; his mother lived there. She was one of the Women.

Dylan opened the sliding glass doors and we went outside. We stood in the dark garden; the air was cool. The light from the swimming pool cast a blue glow around us.

"Let's go skinny-dipping." Brad said.

Summer dipped her foot into the water. "It's freezing."

"I thought it was a heated pool," Molly said.

Valerie said she wanted to play a game they played in her high school in Texas, called Spin the Bottle and Ten Minutes in the Closet. We didn't have a closet, so instead we used the cabana by the pool.

We used an empty seltzer bottle. The bottle pointed to Dylan and between Valerie and Summer. "It's definitely pointing more to Summer," Dylan said.

Dylan walked to Summer, holding his hand out to her. Valerie watched them walk off in the direction of the cabana.

"It was in the middle," she said, sounding upset.

"Dylan has always been in love with Summer," Molly told her. Molly looked at her wristwatch. "I'm timing them."

After ten minutes Dylan and Summer emerged from the cabana, holding hands. Summer looked down at the ground shyly as they walked toward us and took their places in the circle.

The next spin of the bottle landed on Valerie and Sati.

"If a girl gets a girl you can spin again," Brad said.

"I'll go with Valerie," Sati said. Valerie's face lit up. Her white teeth shone in the dark and she jumped up, following Sati to the cabana.

"See?" Dylan said to Brad. "I told you she was a lesbo."

The pool was the color of turquoise and the water looked clear and still. We could hear the soft gurgling sound of the filter and the crickets at night.

"This game sucks," Brad said.

"It's really boring and I'm getting cold," Molly said. "What do you think they're doing in there?"

We looked toward the cabana. More than ten minutes had already gone by, but they had not come out.

"Should I go and get them?" I asked.

"Sure, if you want to," Brad said. As I walked toward the cabana, I could hear their voices. Sati and Valerie were sitting together in the small changing room, with the towels and floats.

"Hi," I said awkwardly. "We were thinking about going back inside."

Valerie looked up at me, she held her arm around her knees and I could see that she had taken off her shirt. They sat facing each other on the wooden bench, with their knees and toes touching.

"We'll be out in a few minutes," Sati said. They were waiting for me to leave.

When they came out they were giddy, laughing as though they were drunk. They had discovered something amazing, they told us. They both had the same birthday, but Valerie was born one year earlier. And they both had the same favorite song, "The Rose."

They stood at the edge of the swimming pool, singing the song together, harmonizing the highs and lows, with the blue light from the pool behind them.

TWENTY-ONE

At breakfast the next morning, Brad and Dylan reenacted the most violent scenes from the movie. Dylan bit into an apple as though it were a neck. Sati and Valerie sat next to each other, leaning forward with laughter.

After breakfast Sati and Valerie walked ahead of us to the classroom, still practicing their duet of "The Rose." I lingered behind with Summer and Molly, trying to think of things to say to distract myself from Sati and Valerie. We walked to school, still dressed up, in the outfits we had worn to Parvati's sleepover.

In the classroom, Kelly handed out a list of vocabulary words we had to study for the ERBs. Kelly told us that Parvati wanted the students to perform well on them. Next fall, the school building would be finished and she wanted it to have a strong reputation. She wanted the students to be accepted at the best colleges.

From the classroom window, I saw Keshi outside, walking with Eden. She held his hand, and I could see that he was crying.

"I think Eden's been hurt," I said, looking at them.

Keshi stood on the porch, still holding Eden's hand. His face was wet, streaming with tears.

"Eden, what happened?" I asked.

"I need to talk to you, May," Keshi said.

Kelly stood at the door with us. "Is everything all right?" she asked, holding the vocabulary sheets in her hand.

"Everything will be fine," Keshi said.

As we walked down the porch steps, Keshi turned back and whispered something to Kelly. Kelly covered her mouth with her hand and her eyes got wide with worry.

"What's the matter, Keshi?" I asked, as we walked away.

From the classroom window, I saw the girls standing beside Kelly, watching us.

"I'll explain what has happened somewhere more private," Keshi said to me.

It was a cool day and I crossed my arms in front of me as Eden and I walked, watching the hem of Keshi's skirt move forward and backward against her legs and the blur of the ground beneath.

We went into Parvati's house and sat down on the benches in the waiting area; there was no one else inside. Keshi sat across from us. She ran her hand over the patterns of seashells printed on her skirt.

"Last night you told us your mother had taken Jaya from the nursery," Keshi said.

I nodded, but I was thinking, Sati told you that.

"Parvati thought she could trust your mother and gave her the privilege of taking care of her daughter." Keshi spoke slowly. She looked from me to Eden. "Unfortunately, your mother broke that trust, and Parvati has made her leave the ashram."

I thought Keshi was saying good-bye to us, that we would be leaving. I thought she had brought us here to say good-bye to Parvati.

I looked at Eden; his eyes looked red, sore.

"Parvati asked your mother to leave last night," Keshi said.

"She's gone?" I knew our mother wouldn't leave without us. "When is she coming back?"

"That's up to Parvati to decide," Keshi said. The calmness of her voice, her hand on the bench was irritating me.

"Please tell me how long," I said loudly, impatiently.

"May," Keshi said, to calm me, "I don't know."

Eden held his hand against his throat. "Where did she go?"

Through the window, the sun shone golden against the green leaves of the trees.

Keshi shook her head. "We don't know."

"Why didn't she tell us herself?"

"You were with Parvati," Keshi said. She leaned forward and put her hands on Eden's knees. "I can see that you're upset," she said, looking at me too. "Parvati wants you to know that we are here for you. We're one big family here, and we will take care of you. You know that, don't you?"

Eden nodded.

"Good," Keshi said. "I'll be here; come and talk to me whenever you want. Okay? You know what I'll do?" She looked at Eden, and her face brightened. "I'll make you your own batch of oatmeal cookies. I'll put extra honey in them. Would you like that?"

Eden didn't answer.

Keshi looked at her watch. "Now you better go to your chores. I'll walk you to the garden, Eden."

When I arrived at the stables, Sati was already there. She was cutting the twine from the hay bales and hadn't heard me come in. Her hair fell straight, covering the side of her face, as she spread the hay on the ground.

The radio was playing, on the shelf where the brushes and tack were kept. Sati sang along to the song. She had a pretty, simple voice, like a child's.

I stood for a moment in the doorway, watching her. The smell of hay mixed with the air.

"Sati?" I said.

She didn't look at me.

"Sati?" I said again. I could tell, by the busy way she moved her hands and the way she hid her face behind her hair, that she knew I was there.

In London my mother had taken me to visit one of her friends. The friend, she told me, had a daughter my age who I could play with. When we arrived at the house, my mother introduced me to her friend's daughter and left me standing in the doorway of the girl's bedroom while she went to talk to her friend in the kitchen.

The girl sat on the floor playing with her dollhouse, a half circle of miniature furniture and dolls around her. She never looked up or spoke to me, and I spent the afternoon sitting on the end of her bed, twisting the button on my cardigan, waiting for her to say hello.

I walked over to Sati and touched her shoulder. I felt her body stiffen.

"Should I give the horses fresh water?" I asked. I didn't know what else to say.

"I already have." Sati took two handfuls of hay and spread them on the stable floor.

Through the barn doors, I could see into the field where the horses grazed. A girl in the field was brushing one of the horses. The girl was Valerie. I stared at her, through the shaded barn, into the light field.

"Valerie's brushing one of the horses."

Sati looked out to the field. "She's brushing Vishnu."

"I have to talk to you," I said, and she turned around, looking at me for the first time. "Parvati made my mother leave the ashram because of what you told her last night."

"I'm sorry," she said. "I didn't know Parvati would make her leave."

Sati went back to spreading the hay across the stable floor. I stood watching her, not knowing what to do or say.

"I don't know why you told her. She was only trying to help your sister and your mother."

"I had to tell her, May," she said.

I stood looking at Sati, waiting, hoping she would say something else to me.

Valerie walked across the field toward us.

"I finished brushing the horses," Valerie said to Sati.

"Thanks," Sati said. They looked at each other, then at me.

Valerie sat down on the hay bale, her legs straight in front of her and her head tilted back, looking up at Sati. She was wearing a pale blue terry-cloth one-piece that zipped up the front.

Sati looked at her. "Should we go? I told Dylan and Brad we'd meet them in the tree house."

"I'm ready," Valerie said. Sati reached for her hand, pulling her up from where she was sitting.

"Bye, May." Sati waved. "You don't have to stay; we did everything. Just remember to close the gate properly. Boxer's learned how to open it."

"All right," I said.

I stood in the barn, watching them walk away. I felt a weakness in my face and bones, a crumbling, shaky feeling, as though I would fall. As though I had to grab something, hold on to something, a branch, the air, even my own hand, to keep from falling.

I went back to our room to see if our mother had left us a letter or a note. I looked on the shelves and on the bed, but there was nothing there.

I lay down on the bed, turning my face to the side and putting my hands beneath the pillow. I thought when I breathed deeply I could smell her, our mother. A smell so familiar to me, in the air and sheets, mixing together on my skin.

"May?" Eden came into the room. He sat down beside me on the edge of the bed. "When do you think she'll come back?"

"I don't know." I felt the weight of my head against the pillow.

Through the window, the sky was nearly dark. I lay on the bed, looking out at it, and Eden sat beside me without speaking. We could hear voices in the hallway and the opening and closing of doors. The soft sound of a song came through the wall of the room next to ours.

There was a knock on the door and I sat up.

"Who is it?" I said.

"It's Keshi. Can I come in?" She opened the door. "I didn't see you in the dining hall, so I brought you some food."

She handed us each a plate wrapped in foil and a fork and napkin.

"Thanks," I said.

I put the plate down on the table beside the bed, next to the fork and napkin.

"Are you hungry, Eden?" I asked, but he only shook his head.

"I made you the cookies. They're in my bag," Keshi said, but she did not give them to him. She stood just inside the doorway. I looked up at her, wondering when she would leave, but she stood watching us.

"Did you find out anything else about our mother?"

"No," Keshi said. "I haven't."

Keshi took a step into the room and closed the door behind her. "Parvati thinks that while your mother is away, Eden should stay with Jabe and his mother."

"I can take care of him," I said.

"Please can I stay with May?" he said.

"We really think it's better if he's with an adult. Why don't you pack a bag of clothes, Eden, and I'll walk over there with you. Jabe's mother will take care of you while your mom is away."

"Tonight?" Eden looked over at me.

"Just take some clothes and your toothbrush, Eden," I told him.

Eden stood up. He walked self-consciously across the room to the closet, where he stood, looking at his clothes. He picked a sweatshirt and a pair of shorts from the shelf. He moved slowly, as though he was unsure of what he was doing.

"Do you have a bag to put them in?" Keshi asked him.

"I have my rucksack." He picked his rucksack off the floor, emptying out the things that were in it. He put the clothes in the bag. He took his toothbrush from the cup on the shelf and a book he had brought from London to read on the airplane but had not yet begun.

"Is that all you need?" Keshi asked him.

Eden nodded.

"Simplicity," she said, in a singsong voice, "is a beautiful thing." She took the oatmeal cookies from her bag. "We can take these to Jabe and his mom as a gift."

Eden held the package in his hand. The light from the ceiling reflected on the foil.

"I'll see you in the morning," I said to him. "At breakfast."

He was only going to the house next door, but something in the way Keshi watched us as we said good-bye made it seem as though I would not see him for a long time.

When they were gone, I cried, pressing my face into the pillow so no one would hear. Later, when it was quiet in the hallway, I opened my bedroom door and went to the bathroom. I didn't want to be alone, but there was no one I wanted to see in this house. In the bathroom I washed my face and brushed my teeth. I looked at myself in the mirror, to see if I had changed since we had been here.

Eden and I had spent time away from our mother before: a summer with Grandfather in Scotland, Easter week at Nanny Hannah's flat in Maida Vale. We had spent time away from our mother and time away from our father, but we had never lived apart from each other.

TWENTY-TWO

I woke early the next morning, before it was light outside. I knew what I had to do. I took the suitcase from the closet and stood on it, reaching for a book on the top shelf. Inside the book were two ten-pound notes. It was some of the money I had taken from my father's shop. I had thought I would change the pounds for American dollars at the bank and buy some American clothes, but we had never gone to a bank.

Eden had a coin collection. He kept it in a plastic bag, hidden in a pocket of the suitcase. When I found the bag, I sat down on the floor of our room and counted the change. There was five dollars and seventy-five cents. That will be enough, I thought. If our mother doesn't come back tonight, that will be enough.

In darshan that evening, Eden thought he saw our mother. "May," he whispered to me, "I think that's Mum over there."

He pointed through the crowded room to a woman sitting near the front. We could not see her face, only her back. Her brown hair was pulled into a low ponytail and she wore an orange shawl with Indian words printed on it. It was the shawl Parvati had given her.

The whole evening, Eden and I watched her, waiting for her to look to the side, to raise her hand, to ask Parvati a question, to make a sound, even a cough, so we would know if it was our mother.

When darshan ended, the woman stood up and turned to the side, talking to the person beside her. She looked nothing like Mum. Except for the color of her hair and the orange shawl, there was no resemblance at all. As I walked out into the night, I wondered how I could have let myself think, let myself believe, that she was our mother.

I made a plan to meet Eden at the stables. It was Sunday, and I knew no one would be there. I gave the horses extra carrots, and they followed me to the fence.

I stroked Boxer's long velvety nose. He smelled like hay, and I felt his warm breath on the inside of my wrist. He had been rescued from a horse farm in Jackson and still had scars on his skin from where he had been burned with cigarettes and cigars by the men who owned him before. There were so many dark scars on his back, it seemed as though they had used him as an ashtray.

He had been an expensive horse when he was young and the man had paid a large amount of money for him, but as he grew, he developed problems with his joints and was not a fast runner. So they kept him inside and took out their frustrations on him. This is what happens to animals: taken from their mothers, bred for money, used, sold, passed around; no one cares.

Boxer had a good life now, a safe place with clean water and pasture, but he would always have a frightened look in his eyes. I tried to kiss him, but he moved away too quickly hitting my chin and I bit my tongue.

The sun felt warm, pressing against my cheeks, and I leaned my head against the wooden fence. On the grass lay a dark-green canvas bag Mum used for shopping in London. In it was a glass jar of water, a flashlight, and some food I had taken from the dining hall. I'd found the flashlight in the stables, on a shelf where the riding helmets were kept. When I turned it on, it lit up a dark corner of the cupboard.

Eden ran across the grass. "Sorry I'm late," he said, when he was near.

"You didn't tell Jabe, did you?"

Eden shook his head.

"Or anyone else?"

"No." He squinted from the sun. He wore his navy gym shorts with the name of his school in London on them, his plimsolls, and a T-shirt he'd grown too tall for. He had his rucksack on his shoulders, and in his hand he held a small plastic compass that he had won in a Christmas cracker last year.

"I packed a picnic," I said.

Eden's skin had turned golden brown, and the bones in his shoulders poked through his shirt. Before we came here, his face had been rounder, the tops of his arms pudgy. Now he looked thinner, older, more like a boy than a child.

"Do you have the flashlight?" he asked.

"Yes. It's in my bag."

Eden adjusted the straps on his rucksack and pulled up his socks to his knees.

We walked across the dry field into the grapefruit grove. It was cooler in the shade of the trees, and a slight breeze came through. Eden reached to pick a grapefruit that was hanging from a low branch. He peeled it, dropping the pale yellow rind on the ground as he walked.

We followed the shallow river to the end of the grove where two pickup trucks were parked, the backs stacked high with wooden crates. We waited to see if anyone was around and to make sure no one had seen us.

We took off our shoes and walked across the river to the other side. I pushed the bushes away, but behind them was a tall barbed-wire fence. I could see that it ran around the grove.

"There's a fence," I said. "Sati didn't tell me there was a fence."

"We can crawl under it."

Eden held the bottom wire up, but it was fastened so tightly to the posts he could not pull it very high. The wire caught my hair as I crawled beneath and scraped me through my shirt. Then I held the wire up for him.

"Which way do we go now?" Eden asked, when we were both on the other side.

"We just follow the river. It leads right to the petrol station, I think."

As we walked farther into the woods, I remembered the things our grandfather had taught us. He told us, when we were in the Scottish woods, to remember markers—a fallen tree or a large stone —and always look at the position of the sun in the sky.

I remembered something else too. On one of our walks through the woods, I had heard a whimpering sound, like a baby's cry. A young fox had been caught by the leg in a trap. He had tried to free himself by chewing off his foot, and the trap and the grass below were red with his blood.

I thought of Sati walking all this way alone to telephone her grandparents. The river was shallow from lack of rain and the banks were dry where the water had once been.

We came to an abandoned campsite. Stones circled a fire pit; faded beer cans and rifle cartridges lay scattered across the ground. Eden and I sat down in the clearing and unpacked the food we had brought with us. He pulled out two red tomatoes and gave one to me. I had made peanut-butter sandwiches and brought out a napkin full of almonds and raisins.

I wondered how many miles we had walked and suddenly felt tired and wanted to lay my head down on the canvas bag and close my eyes for a few minutes. Last night, thinking about leaving the ashram, I had not been able to fall asleep.

We finished eating and threw the crusts into the trees. We

stood up, wiping the dirt and leaves from the bottom of our shorts. As we were walking away, I saw something on the ground and stopped to pick it up; it was Eden's compass. Last year, at Christmas, we had fought over a cracker, but Eden broke off the larger end and won: the prize, the joke, and the crown too.

We continued on for a mile or two, following the river through the woods. Then we saw the petrol sign above the treetops, turning in the clear blue sky.

In the convenience store at the petrol station, we wandered the aisles, choosing which soda and candy we wanted to buy. I carried the green bag over my shoulder, but held my polka-dot purse in my hand.

I paid with the change from Eden's coin collection. The shop-keeper was an old man, wearing a baseball cap. His hands shook as he counted out the change.

"Is this your shop?" Eden asked the man.

He looked up, surprised by the question. "No," he said. "I only work here."

"Oh," Eden said, sounding disappointed. "I was only asking because my dad has a shop too."

The man smiled at Eden and gave him a piece of bubble gum from a jar on the counter. We said good-bye and the man waved. When I looked back at the shop, he was still looking at us through the window.

We sat on a bench outside. I ate the pieces of candy one at a time and felt the sweetness cutting against the roof of my mouth. Eden sipped his soda and ate his chocolate bar; he swung his feet forward and backward beneath the bench.

When we finished our sweets, we walked across the empty parking lot to the pay phone. The change in my hand felt heavy, damp with sweat. I lifted the receiver, which was warm, and pressed zero.

An American operator answered. I told her I wanted to call London, England, and she said she would have to connect me to the international operator. I waited, staring at the numbers.

Eden kicked a piece of gravel with the toe of his shoe.

The international operator came on the line; she said I would need to deposit three dollars and seventy-five cents for the first three minutes.

"Three dollars and seventy-five cents," I said back to her. "I don't have enough change."

I didn't have enough change left, after buying the sodas and sweets. I never thought it would cost that much. I looked at the shop, wondering if the old man would loan us a dollar.

A car drove into the petrol station and stopped in front of the shop. Two women got out wearing halter tops and shorts. One walked into the shop while the other filled the car up at the pump.

We would have to call our father collect, and our father hated collect calls.

I watched the woman fill her car up. She held the pump in one hand and rested the other hand on her hip. Her brown hair was feathered back. She looked very confident, almost tough. Her friend came from the shop, and the woman holding the pump laughed, slapping her thigh at something her friend said.

"I'll have to phone him collect," I said.

"Remember the time Mum phoned him collect from Spain and he got really cross?"

"Yes, Eden, I remember."

I knew exactly the time he was talking about and wished he hadn't reminded me. We had taken the boat to Spain to visit Mum's friend, Suzy, who had rented a villa for the summer with her sister and her sister's boyfriend. The house was in a small mountain village with no telephone or running water. In the mornings we walked down the mountain to a café in the village, where we ate warm fresh rolls with butter and jam. Mum had café con leche and Eden and I drank steamed milk with a drop of espresso or chocolate for flavor. One morning, at breakfast in the café, Mum said. "Simon would love it here, don't you think? Let's phone him and convince him to leave the shop for a few days and come and spend the rest of the holiday with us."

She paid the bill and asked for directions to the public telephone. Inside the red phone booth, in the village square, she pressed the receiver to her ear. "Collect, *por favor,*" she said, smiling at us because she knew she sounded funny. Her face lit up when he picked up the phone.

"Simon, I'm so glad you picked up. It's us, we're calling from—"

But the first thing he said was "Collect? Is this an emergency? This is costing me a bloody fortune."

Mum hung up the telephone without telling him why she was calling. The excitement had left her face, and she looked shaken. She stood for a while in the phone booth with her back to us while we waited outside, watching the children play football in the village square.

I could feel my pulse beating in my fingertip as I pressed zero to phone collect.

"Operator."

"Hello. I'd like to make a collect call to London, England."

"Hold please," she said. The international operator had a northern accent. I imagined her sitting at a desk in a long room, wearing headphones and a pleated skirt.

"We're trying to reach our father," I explained, but she was only interested in his telephone number.

"Hold the line while I place your call." There was an echo down the line and I heard the telephone ringing. The telephone was ringing in the kitchen of our house. I imagined our father, sitting up in bed or standing up from the table, walking slowly, casually, across the room. Porridge, asleep on the kitchen chair, would hear it too, lifting her head from her paws.

There was a click and the operator's voice. "The answer-phone picked up. You can try your call later."

When she said later, it sounded like *layta*.

"Can I leave a message?"

"Sorry, not on a collect call. If you call direct you can leave a message."

"Oh, I know, but we don't have enough—" I said, but she had already disconnected us.

"What happened?" Eden asked, touching my arm.

"He didn't answer. He must not be at home. She said to try later."

We stood by the pay phone, looking out at the parking lot. A man driving a pale silver-colored car pulled into the petrol station. He drove slowly, his head turning to look at us as he parked.

Eden and I walked across the lot, back to the bench, waiting for *later*. Eden picked up a handful of gravel. He aimed the stones at a metal garbage can. He was talking excitedly about the things he was going to do when he got back to London.

The man stepped out of the car and put his keys in the front pocket of his jeans. He was in his twenties with short brown hair and a handsome face. He saw me looking at him as he walked into the shop and smiled.

"Who is that man?" Eden said.

"I don't know."

"Why did he smile at you?"

"I don't know, Eden."

"I have to pee."

"Well, go behind a tree."

Eden walked behind the shop and into the woods. The morning had been warm, but now a cooler breeze was coming in. I had only worn an old white T-shirt, shorts, and sandals, and now, sitting in the sun, there were goose bumps on my arms.

The man who had smiled at me walked out of the shop with a packet of cigarettes in his hand. He looked both ways as the door closed behind him. As he walked toward the bench where I was sitting, he unwrapped the cellophane from the cigarettes and let it fall to the ground.

"Hey," he said, cupping his hand to light his cigarette, but there was a breeze and he had to turn away. "The weather's getting cooler," he said, looking at me.

I nodded. "Yeah, it is."

"Do you smoke?"

"Sure."

In London, Greta had taught me to inhale and exhale properly. She said it was a good thing to learn, before I started going out to the clubs.

He handed me a cigarette. The tip of his finger touched mine. I could see him looking at me and I liked his attention. I thought, as I held the cigarette to my lips, this would make me feel better, a man, a boyfriend to make me forget about Sati.

"Need a light?" He cupped his hand over mine to light it. He had muscular arms. Beneath the cigarette smoke I could smell his cologne.

"Thanks," I said, inhaling.

"Nice accent. Australian?"

I shook my head; the smoke was caught in my throat. "No, English."

"Are you here for vacation?" When he squinted, the corners of his eyes creased. In the sun, he looked older. He spoke in a gentle voice, his light brown hair was thinning on top. There was a softness about him. His eyes were so pale, they looked as though they would disintegrate in the bright light.

"Yeah, we're just visiting," I said.

"Where are you staying?"

"Rosemont."

"Rosemont? There's not much going on there. Have you been to Filmore?"

I shook my head. His eyes went from my face, to my chest, to the road. He smiled at me as he described the beaches in Filmore, long beaches with soft white sand and the waves great for surfing. I turned my body toward him on the bench, crossing one leg over the other, straightening, pulling my shoulders back. I exhaled with my mouth halfway open, the way I had seen Greta do.

I wanted to ask him if he thought I was pretty, if that's why he was talking to me. It was a question inside—why Sati chose Valerie and left me—and I thought he could tell me the answer. A stranger, who I would never see again.

"My apartment looks right at the ocean," he said. "I wake up in the morning, and the first thing I see is the Pacific. It's amazing. You should come see it while you're here."

"Yeah," I said. I imagined myself standing on his terrace, looking out at dark-blue waves.

"Hey, you look like you're getting cold." He leaned forward and put his hand on my leg, close to the edge of my shorts. I felt the heat from his palm against my thigh. I knew what this would feel like now. We sat behind the shop; there was no one else around. I opened my legs, slightly, unsure. He looked at me, surprised. His hand moved under the hem of my shorts; his fingers grazed the edge of my underwear.

"Do you need a ride somewhere?" His voice was almost a whisper.

I shook my head, moving my leg away from his hand. "My brother just went to get something. We're waiting for our father to pick us up."

He held his hand still, his fingers pressing firmly against my underwear. The soft expression in his eyes had changed. It was as though he were looking though a telescope at me, with a hardened focus.

"You look really cold," he said softly.

I tried to close my legs, but his hand pressed against my thigh. There was no one except for the old man who worked inside the shop, and I couldn't see him from where I sat.

I saw Eden, walking from the trees, studying the compass in his hand. The man took his hand from my thigh, slowly, as though he were wiping something from them.

"Just trying to be helpful." He put the packet of cigarettes in the front pocket of his shirt. "By the way, my name's Jack." He held his hand out for me to shake. I didn't want to, but I held my hand out to him. "What's yours?"

"Alice." I crossed my arms in front of me.

"Alice, pretty name. Well, see you around, Alice." I sat on the bench, watching him walk to his car. He got in and closed the door. He turned the engine on but did not drive away.

"What took you so long?" I stood up.

Eden shrugged. "Nothing." He sat down next to me on the bench and the man drove out of the parking lot, his car disappearing down the road.

"Should we try phoning him again?"

"Yeah."

We stood up from the bench. I thought, as we walked past the place where the man's car had been, that I could smell his cologne in the air.

I picked up the telephone receiver, but this time the excitement was gone, and the phone felt heavy in my hand. The operator said there was still no answer. I put the receiver down. The sun was setting below the trees and the yellow and orange light was fading.

Eden and I walked for a while by the side of the river, in the shaded woods. I felt the wind on my arms and through my shirt. "It's getting dark," Eden said. "Do you have the flashlight?"

I opened my shoulder bag and took out the flashlight. A circle of light shone against the ground, lighting up the earth and leaves. We walked on, shining the light—on the river, across the trees—but soon the beam became dim, and the circle grew smaller.

"The light's fading," Eden said. He switched it off, waiting a few minutes before turning it on again.

"But it was just working."

I took it from him, shaking it. When I found it, on the shelf with the riding helmets, the light had seemed so bright in the dark cupboard, lighting up the dusty shelves and the back wall where a couple had carved their names in the wood.

"It was working before," I said.

I turned it off and on again, but it only flickered and dimmed. Eden and I stared silently at the ground, watching the circle of light growing smaller and smaller. As the light faded, it seemed as though the sounds of the woods became louder: the scrape of pines and twigs beneath our feet, the shallow running water of the river.

"What are we going to do?" Eden said.

I shook my head. It was too dark, I thought, to try to find our way back through the woods. We were not far from the road, but if we walked alongside it, we took the chance of being seen by someone from the ashram.

The idea of being lost in the dark woods made me panic.

"We have to walk along the road," I said, hurrying ahead, stumbling over the low branches, moving forward out of the woods. If I had stayed, one moment longer, if the light of the torch had died and I had let my eyes adjust to the darkness, I would have seen that the moonlight shaded by the trees was bright enough for us to have made our way along the river.

There were no streetlights on the road, only the nearly full moon, shining above. A car went by and then another, and then there were none for a long time and the road was quiet. The broken yellow line glowed under the moonlight.

"Maybe we can try to telephone him another day," Eden said hopefully, his voice rising like a bird.

I stumbled on a piece of asphalt that had broken from the side of the road. What had I thought? I thought we would leave the ashram to telephone our father and he would be sitting at home by the phone, waiting for our call. "Hello?" he would say. I imagined his voice, like lightning, down the telephone line.

We heard the sound of a car behind us and moved over to the side of the road. The car slowed as it passed us, I felt its headlights shining against my back. I thought, It's someone from the ashram. I thought, We've been caught.

"Hey, Alice," a man's voice said, and I turned around. "Hey, it's me, Jack." He leaned his head out of the window. "Your ride didn't show up?"

I looked behind at the road, wondering if he had followed us. "I was just on my way home," he said. "I thought I should offer you a ride." A song was playing on the car radio, and for a moment I found myself straining to hear the words.

"Why didn't your dad show up?" he asked, frowning, looking concerned.

From the corner of my eye, I saw Eden standing near me. He stood completely still, as if he were afraid to move.

The man let out a slight laugh. There was something different about him now, a piercing look in his eyes. "I know what you two are," he said. "You're runaways."

I shook my head. "No," I said. "No, we're not."

"Well, if you're not running away, why don't you get in and I'll give you a ride home? You shouldn't be walking alone in the dark. I'll give you a ride, anywhere. Anywhere you want to go, just let me know." He smiled a wide friendly smile.

I looked ahead at the road. The night had grown cooler and the walk back to the ashram seemed long. The road was empty and quiet. It would be easy for us to get into his car, for him to drive us the few miles to the ashram gates and let us out there. We would be warm and maybe there would still be some food left over from dinner. Maybe he was just being friendly; everyone knows Americans are helpful, friendly people.

As I looked away from the road, back to the man, a new song came on the car radio and he turned the volume up, so the music spilled out of his car windows and into the night. I remember thinking, Someone will hear us.

"I love this song," he said, as he reached forward, taking something from beneath the seat. The song that was playing had been the summer hit in England. One night, Mum, Eden, and I had all sung along to it in the kitchen. That's what I thought of when I heard the song: the three of us, singing in the kitchen of our house.

"Hey, Alice, come here. I want to show you something." He held something I couldn't see clearly in his hand. "Come on over here, take a look."

I felt myself walk toward him; the sense of being a girl, the sense of being polite. How could I refuse to look at what he wanted to show me? I just wanted to be calm and for him to drive away. But I had the feeling as I walked away from Eden that I had made a mistake, that a rope had been broken.

When I was near the car window, he turned his headlights off and the road went dark. "Come on, Alice don't be a tease. Get in the car, we'll have a good time together," he whispered. He reached across the passenger seat, pushing open the door. The car was clean inside, empty. Except for a bottle of soda and a newspaper folded next to him on the seat, there was nothing else.

I looked back at Eden. He was standing where I had left him, his hand clenched around the hem of his shorts. From where I stood, I could see the straps of his rucksack over his shoulders. It was so familiar to me; we had walked together to school every morning in London. I wished we were there now, on our street, at the bus stop, looking in the window of Tiger, Tiger, waiting for the bus to take us to school. All the times I had seen him wearing his rucksack, I never thought we would ever be alone on a highway in California in the night. I suddenly felt sick in my stomach.

The man twisted a piece of cloth between his hands. "It's warm inside," he said. "And you sure look cold."

He had said this before, at the petrol station. Hearing it again annoyed me.

"I'm not cold."

He said, softly, "I can see your nipples through your shirt."

I looked down at my shirt. I hadn't noticed how thin the cotton had become. When I looked up, he was grinning at me through the open window. "It looks sexy on a young girl. It's a real turn-on."

I held the broken flashlight in my hand. He moved toward me across the car seat, pushing a soda bottle and newspaper away. "Get in, Alice," he said. When he reached to touch me, I threw the flashlight at his face.

"What the fuck?" He held his hand over his left eye. "What the fuck did you just do?" He picked up the flashlight from his lap. "You little bitch!" he yelled. "What did you do that for?" He touched his face again, flinching, as though he were in pain.

I stepped back, away from the car.

He took his hand from the side of his face, looking at his reflection in the rearview mirror. He touched his eyebrow, lifting his chin. I saw Eden, watching with a wide frightened look in his eyes. The man pushed open his car door and I stepped back again. He stood up, leaning his forehead against the door frame for a moment, as though he were dizzy. He walked around the car, opening his trunk and taking something from it.

I listened for the sound of other cars, but there were none. Then he walked toward me, his footsteps soft on the road.

"May, come on!" Eden called. He had walked farther away from the car, down the slope at the side of the road to where the woods began. I ran toward him, following him into the woods. When I looked back, I saw the man running after us, down the shallow slope to the trees. Leaving his car, with the radio still playing, by the side of the road.

As we ran through the woods, tree branches scraped our arms and legs. Eden stumbled, falling forward; he pushed himself up, running deeper into the woods. I was thinking as I ran: he'll hear our footsteps over the dry ground; he'll see my white T-shirt, like a light, in the dark.

I didn't know which way we were running, to the road or away from it. Where was the river? Insects flew in my mouth and eyes. Everything mixed together in a blur, the ground and the sky. I thought I could hear his footsteps behind me; I thought I could even hear his breath. Don't look back, don't look back, I told myself; it takes time away from running. But I couldn't help it and I stopped for a moment, standing still, to listen.

The man came from behind me. He grabbed my hair and my neck jerked back. He put one arm around my waist and his other hand covered my mouth and nose. There was a metallic taste on his fingers. I tried to push his hand away; I was trying to breathe.

He pushed me to the ground. "Why did you do that?" he yelled. "I was just being friendly."

He put his hands inside my shorts, pressing roughly with his hands. He put his hand between my legs. His fingernails scraped inside me. I swung my arm around, trying to get him away. I tried to run from him but I fell forward with my face against the ground.

Everything went dark around me and I thought I had fallen down a hole. I grabbed at the dirt, but it crumbled in my hands. I felt the man's body against me, pushing my face into the ground. I couldn't catch my breath. It was like rolling under a wave in stormy seawater, thick with sand and stones.

His fingers pulled my hair, and with his other hand he grabbed the back of my shirt, turning me over onto my back. He stood over me, taking the piece of cloth from his jacket pocket. He pushed my shoulders against the ground and put his knees against my thighs. I turned away from him, but he pushed me back and my head hit against the ground.

His forehead was damp with sweat and his breathing was heavy, almost labored. He held his hands against my shoulders, looking down at me. He seemed suddenly confused. He looked up, taking his hands from my shoulders as though he had suddenly heard his name called. He looked behind him into the woods. He stood up quickly and ran through the woods, in the direction of the road.

I lay on the ground.

The sound of his footsteps grew farther away, until I could no longer hear them. I lay in the place he had left me as though waiting for him to return. When I pushed myself up, there was a sharp pain in my ribs and a throbbing in my head.

"Eden?" I called, staring into the trees.

I thought of the man's face, turning, changing color. The way the sky might suddenly brighten or darken. Had he heard a sound? Realized that he had left his car on the road? Had he heard Eden? Seen him? Had he run to get him instead of me? There was a beating in my chest, a feeling that I thought would never settle.

"May? Where are you?" It was Eden's voice.

"I'm here." I said, but could not see him. "Eden?"

"Yes."

I imagined that the man had him. That this was a trap. Then I saw Eden standing in the woods and I ran toward him.

I held him in my arms, his head touching beneath my chin. I held him close. I felt his arms around me, holding me tight, the warmth between our bodies like a line.

"Let's go," he said. "Let's go." Eden pulled my hand, trying to make me leave this place, where the man had been.

"What did he do to you?" Eden asked.

I shook my head. "He pushed me down. Then he didn't do anything." The sound of the words surprised me. I wouldn't tell him that he had touched me.

"Do you think he'll come back?"

"I don't know."

I took Eden's hand and we walked quickly, farther into the woods. The night was growing colder and I could feel Eden shivering beside me. I was thinking, Parvati, keep us safe. It was the first time I had said these words, and through the night they repeated in my head like a prayer.

Mosquitoes and insects buzzed around us. I heard a sound, a rustle in the trees.

"What's that?" Eden whispered.

We stood still, listening. Two deer ran through the trees, flashing like brown lights, then disappeared. Eden was still, watching them. This is what I thought it must feel like, to be as frightened as a deer. There was nothing to be afraid of; no animal or insect would harm us. The only thing to fear was the man, hiding, watching us, waiting —we didn't know where.

We heard the shallow sound of the river near us and followed alongside it. As we walked, the woods seemed to brighten around us, as though we were holding a candle, but it was only the light from the moon, falling in patches through the trees. We walked quickly, without speaking, as though we knew our way.

In the damp night air we could smell the grapefruit. We crawled beneath the barbed wire, into the ashram and I knew we were safe. I felt my shoulders relax. We walked between the lines of planted trees, past the fort where Sati used to play. I breathed in the bitter smell of the grapefruit. I wouldn't tell anyone. I thought of myself opening my legs, the man's fingers on my shorts, and I turned away from the thought, as though turning away from the mirror. I would not tell anyone. Not yet. Not for a long time. I did not want this to be a part of me, part of my life.

"Eden," I said. "You mustn't tell anyone."

"Even Mum?"

I shook my head. I could not tell our mother.

"No, Eden. Do not tell anyone. Please don't."

He was silent for a moment. "All right," he said. "I won't."

As we passed the stables and the still, dark figures of the horses in the field, we could see the shape of the houses, and the lights inside the windows. I thought, by now, someone would be looking for us. Jabe and his mother would be looking for Eden. "Jabe's mother will be looking for you," I said. "Say you were searching the woods for wood for the fort or something . . . that's where you got the bug bites and scratches."

Eden nodded. He stood listening, as though to instructions, with an attentive look on his face. I imagined I saw a deepness set in his eyes. I thought, The next time I look, in a different day, in a different light, a different room, it will be gone. He will look like himself again: like a young boy.

Now in the opening, under the moonlight, I could see the dirt on Eden's clothes, the scrapes from branches on his arms and legs.

"Your face," Eden said. He reached up to touch me but pulled his hand away. I felt my forehead, bulging just above my left eyelid.

Eden said, "You can say you fell from a tree when we were building the fort." I nodded. I would say that I fell from the tree or that I fell while I was running.

We said good-bye outside the house. "Eden," I said. "You have to promise you won't say anything else."

"I won't," he said. I watched him as he walked away, in the dark, along the path.

*   *   *

That night, as I walked up the stairs of the house to our room, I felt something familiar, like a sound or a smell, but couldn't place it. I stood on the stairs, looking down at the carpet, listening to the voices in the living room coming past the lights in the hall.

I ran into the bathroom, locking the door and leaving my clothes on the floor. The torn white T-shirt, my denim shorts, my underpants. I wanted to throw them all away.

In the shower the water stung my thigh: a cut, a fingernail mark from the man. I combed out the knots in my wet hair, roughly, with my fingers. I could hear the sound of my hair breaking at the ends. I brought my wrist to my nose. I thought that even beneath the smell of the soap the smell of the man's cologne lingered, the smell of his body and skin. I felt a sickness at the bottom of my stomach, rising into my chest. I had straightened my back on the bench, I had moved my legs apart, and for a moment I had liked the feeling of his hand on my thigh. I looked at myself in the mirror and turned away.

I dried myself with my shirt and dressed in my old clothes. When the hallway was quiet, I went to the bedroom.

I opened the bedroom door and I saw a woman sitting on the bed in the dark room. She stood up when she saw me.

"Mum?"

The door was half open behind me, and she put her finger in front of her lips.

"Close the door," she whispered. I could see that she was nervous and I turned quickly, closing the door and locking it. I could hear her breath as she stood across the room from me. "Come here, darling."

She walked toward me, and when she was near she put her arms around me, pulling me close to her. "I'm so sorry. I'm so sorry I left you." She held me and I felt the relief of her body next to mine. The smell of her skin, the touch of her hair against my cheek, as familiar to me as a bone in my own body. I wanted to stay like that, for her to hold me, but I pushed her away.

"Why did you leave without telling us?"

"I didn't have a choice."

I remember staring at her, as though it were not Mum but only a photograph of her. A suitcase lay open by the door, and the shelves in the closet were empty.

"Does Parvati know you're here?"

"No. Where's Eden?" my mother asked, suddenly.

"Eden doesn't live here anymore. He lives with Jabe and his mother in Lackshman House."

When I told her this, something changed in her face. Like a blanket slipping from the bed.

"Parvati thought it would be better if he was with an adult."

"How long has he been gone?"

"Since you left."

My mother nodded slowly, as though this was something she understood but had not expected. I bent down to take some clothes from the suitcase, and my mother switched on the light so I could see.

In the light my mother touched the side of my head. "What happened to you?"

"Nothing," I said, and pulled away from her.

She looked at me strangely; the way you might look at some-one you recognize but whose name you had forgotten.

She reached out to touch the side of my face and I flinched. "Tell me what happened to you," she said.

"I fell. I fell while I was climbing the tree to the fort."

Through the hallway, a man called out that it was time for darshan. We heard the front door open and close and from the window the sound of voices rising up, a group of people walking together outside.

TWENTY-THREE

Darshan had already begun. My mother opened the door quietly and we stepped inside the room. The last people in, the latecomers, were not allowed to find a closer spot but had to sit right beside the door.

My mother sat down, with her back to the door. She put her hand to her chest, as though trying to catch her breath.

The room was decorated for Jaya's christening. Vases of white flowers had been placed on the tables. A silver pitcher of water and an empty silver bowl sat on a table next to the chair where Parvati sat. Afterward, Indian sweets would be passed around the room. Trays of the pink-and-white coconut sweets and corn colored balls waited in the kitchen.

The chanting began and Parvati walked into the room, holding the baby in her arms. The baby was dressed in a white antique christening gown. Sati and the Women walked behind Parvati. Sati wore a short floral-print dress; in her hand she held a small bouquet of white flowers.

As Parvati carried Jaya through the room, I saw Caroline and John sit up, trying to catch a glimpse of the baby.

Sati sat beside Parvati, and the candlelight reflected a soft glow on her skin. I wished, for a moment, that I could have believed in Parvati. The belief would have taken me from the rest of the world. Cut the other threads, so that being here with Parvati was the only one that remained. I imagined the simplicity of that feeling, the safety and purpose of it.

In the middle of the room, I saw Eden sitting beside Jabe and his mother. He held his hands together on his lap, his shoulders hunched slightly forward.

Parvati gave the baby to Sati to hold, the trail of white dress falling over her arms. "Namaste, my children," Parvati began. "Tonight is my daughter Jaya's christening." She said she would be christened in all religions, in the way they believed on the ashram in all gods.

Parvati talked about Jaya. She said at three months she was just beginning to smile. She chewed on her fingers, and her favorite toy was a stuffed animal duck she slept with. Sati held up the stuffed animal in front of Jaya, who reached for it, and everyone laughed.

Caroline laughed too, as she sat cross-legged on the floor, holding her husband's hand. She leaned forward, laughing louder than the others in the room, her face red, as though she were on the verge of tears.

My mother stood up. She walked through the crowded room, until she was near the center, where she stood in the dim light. Parvati looked at her from across the room.

"Lucy, my *chela*," she said. "I am happy to see you, but I have not asked you back yet."

"I am not here to ask for your forgiveness. I have come to tell you that we are leaving." I could see she was frightened of Parvati. Afraid that Parvati would sway her, make her stay. I thought, If Sati took my hand in hers, if she wrote *I love you* with her finger down my back, I would want to stay here too.

Parvati looked at her. "I know you are angry."

My mother shook her head. "You are not the guru I want to follow."

It seemed as though a sound like a wave carried through the room. As though our mother were standing in still-churning water.

"This is the best place for your children. What will you take them back to, a bad marriage? To fights and unhappiness? You told me you have never felt satisfied. Is that what you want for your children?"

My mother did not answer. She stood in the room, the gray sweater she wore hanging from her shoulders and her head bowed slightly. I saw her touch her finger to her eyebrow, as though wiping something away. "I don't know what we will be going back to," she said quietly.

"You don't know anything," Parvati said. As though she pitied her, as though she considered her a foolish woman.

My mother looked into the room, searching for Eden. When she saw him, she walked quickly toward him. She reached for Eden's hand, pulling him close to her. "We came to say good-bye," my mother said to Parvati.

"Let me say good-bye to the children," Parvati said.

Eden and I walked toward her across the crowded room. When we reached her she held us tightly in her arms.

"I'll keep you in my heart," she said and let us go.

Sati sat holding the baby. I tried to catch her eye, but she would not look at me. She looked down at Jaya, touching her head with her hand. I waited for a moment, wondering what to say. Would she write? Could I write to her? But she looked down at the baby and did not look back up at me.

Eden said good-bye to Jabe; they stood in front of each other. Jabe leaned into his mother, hiding his tears in her side.

I saw Sumner and Molly watching me, but their faces seemed expressionless.

Parvati asked Renee to walk us to the gates, and as we were leaving she said my mother's name. "Lucy?"

"Yes?"

"Who let you through the gates?"

"Parvati," she said, and I thought I saw a smile form on my mother's lips, "I would never tell you that."

At the door, Caroline and my mother said good-bye. They held each other tightly. "Thank you," my mother whispered into her ear. "I'll miss you."

*   *   *

Outside, the air was cool and the night was dark. Renee walked ahead of us, an arm's length away. Was she embarrassed? Had she failed in front of Parvati, bringing our mother here only to have her decide to leave? Was she disappointed in our mother, returning now to the life she had left behind?

"I have to get the luggage from the room," our mother said to Renee. "I've already packed. I know you want to get back to darshan."

"I do," Renee said.

Inside the room, the shelves were bare. Our things packed in the two suitcases we had come with. A pile of clothes Eden had grown out of sat on the bed.

Eden took his tin of pencils from his bag, the book of plain paper. He handed them to Renee. "I want to give these to Jabe."

"That's nice of you," Mum said to him.

I looked to see what I could leave. I wanted to leave something for Sati. I thought of the photographs her father had taken when Jaya was two days old and wondered if she would miss me when she saw them.

"Is there anything you want me to send you from London?" my mother asked Renee.

Renee shook her head. "I have everything I need here."

My mother picked up the handle of her suitcase. She hesitated by the door. There was a chip in her eye, like the chip in the flower on the blue and white china plate. For a moment, I thought she would change her mind and we would stay here. She looked around at the small bare room. Was this enough for her? The newness she was looking for, the things she had wanted to change, had failed here. I could see in that moment that she still believed in something else, in something more, but understood she would live her life knowing this but never finding it.

I touched my hand to the wall. This would be the last time I saw this room. The last time we walked down the stairs past the spotless bathroom, the kitchen, the living room with its stale smell of incense. Sati had not looked up at me to say good-bye. I wanted to go back to darshan and say good-bye to her again. It felt, in my mind, like untying a knot.

Our Grandmother Hannah always kissed the wall of her house before she left. She kissed the narrow part next to the front door. It was superstitious, but it meant she would return home safely. I wanted to kiss the wall but only lingered with my fingertips before turning off the light and following my mother and Eden downstairs.

We walked along the path to the gates. My mother held the suitcase, dragging it in the sand. Renee helped her with the duffel bag, and Eden and I carried our own luggage.

We stopped inside the gates.

"I'm sorry, Renee," our mother said.

In London, when Renee had sat in the kitchen of our house with Annabel and Suzy, she would admire the house itself, the things inside: the glass vase shaped like a flower, the Indian rug in the living room, the paintings on the walls.

Here as she unlocked the gates, it was as though she was letting us out of her house, a house we had been lucky to be invited to but would not be asked back again.

"I'm sorry too," Renee said. There was a tone in her voice of pity, as she thought of us returning to the place we had left.

Renee unlocked the gates and we walked through them, to the edge of the road. The car our mother had rented was parked along the side. "Let me know you've arrived safely," Renee said.

"I will," she said. They embraced quickly. I looked behind through the gates, to the path leading through the ashram. Eden stood beside Mum, waiting for her to take his hand again.

*　*　*

We sat in the car. Our mother turned the engine key and the car lights lit up the trees and the yellow line on the road. She pulled cautiously into the lane and drove straight onto the highway.

"I'm so sorry I left you," she said, her voice reaching to the front window. "Did anyone tell you what happened?"

"Keshi told us," I said. "Where have you been staying?"

"In a motel."

We drove past the gas station. The lights of the shop were dark now, and there were no cars in the lot.

"We're going back to England," our mother said.

"Tonight?"

"Tomorrow."

"Have you spoken to Dad?"

"Yes. He sent us money for the airplane tickets."

Through the window, the trees on the side of the road blurred. The night was cool, but not cold, and the air came through the opening at the top of the window. I thought of Boxer. I had not said good-bye to him. I would miss the horses. I would miss them so much.

In the motel lobby, a woman sat behind the front desk, talking on the telephone. Music played softly on the radio. A string of tinsel and old Christmas cards hung across the window behind her. It was February.

"Your key?" she asked, covering the mouthpiece with her hand.

"Yes, thank you," our mother said. Her English accent, even her posture, seemed too formal as she spoke to the woman at the desk.

Eden sat down in a burnt-orange-colored chair, looking into the fish tank by the wall. Coffee in a pot sat half full on a burner next to a tray of creamers and sugars and Styrofoam cups.

Our mother held the key in her hand, watching Eden stare into the goldfish tank: the soft gurgling sound of the filter, plastic plants and a mermaid sprouting from a treasure chest, small red and

orange fish swimming between these things. Swimming in the clear
water above the turquoise pebbles. If you looked closely enough,
like Eden, his nose nearly touching the glass, the tank might disappear and it would look like a magical world.

Our mother led us down the carpeted hallway, past a wood-paneled
cigarette machine and a candy machine, to our room.

Inside, the light was on. The bed was made, covered with an
orange-and-red-flecked spread. Her clothes lay at the foot of it. A
glass of water and an open book were on the bedside table. We put
our suitcases inside the door. The air in the room smelled faintly of
cigarette smoke and the air from the road.

A small table sat against a window covered in half curtains.
The lights from cars shone through the fabric as they drove by.

"May," my mother said, walking closer to me. "That bruise is
terrible."

I stepped back, away from her. I didn't want her to touch me.

"I'll get you ice and an aspirin. Something to bring down the
swelling."

She stood in the room looking at Eden and me, as though she
did not know what to do. There was something changed about her,
as if half of her had been replaced by a stranger. The stranger who
had left us without saying good-bye.

Eden sat down on the bed.

"Why didn't you come back and get us? You didn't even tell
us you were leaving or where you went," he said.

"What were you doing here the whole time?" I heard an anger
in my voice I did not recognize.

"I was waiting for Parvati to call and tell me I could come
back," she said flatly. My mother shook her head. Her face looked
faded, tired; she turned up her hands. "Are you two hungry? There's
a diner across the street."

"I'm hungry," Eden said. "We didn't have dinner tonight."

We hadn't eaten since our picnic in the woods. The picnic in the woods near the fire pit seemed confined to a picture frame, a picture of something that had happened many years ago. I looked at Eden, so he would know not to say anything else.

"Let's go across the street. We can bring the food back if you want." She took the keys from the bedside table and put them in her pocket. She took out her purse, counting the money inside.

Eden walked to the small table in the kitchenette, looking out at the cars passing along the road.

"Come on, darling. Eden?"

He turned from the window, as though surprised to hear his name.

"May? Are you coming?"

"I'll just stay here," I said.

"Why don't you come with us? Please come with us." She held the key in the palm of her hand. I could see she didn't want to leave us again, so soon.

"I want to stay here, Mum. I'm tired."

"Okay." She sighed. Eden walked over to her, she took his hand and they left the room. I heard her lock the door behind them.

I sat down on the chair by the window and pulled back the curtain. I watched them walk across the parking lot. The lights from the passing cars crossed over them, bright white, then blue. They stood together at the edge of the double lane, waiting.

The diner sign lit up the sky, a model of a milkshake and a straw flashed in neon lights. Our mother stood at the edge of the road, holding her collar closed with one hand and Eden beside her. In a pause of cars, they ran across the road.

A car pulled into the parking lot below our window. A man with short hair and a zipper-front jacket stepped out. He lit a cigarette, leaning against the car. I imagined I saw him look up at our window with a smile. A smile that said, Got you.

I let go of the curtain, and it fell closed. I went to the door and turned the inside lock and felt a beating in my chest. The lamplight shone a circle of light against the bedspread. I looked at the pictures of the ocean on the walls, of the California surf. Our mother had stayed here for three days. An open packet of cigarettes sat by the telephone. She had sat here, looking at her watch, looking at the phone, picking up the receiver, checking the dial tone. She had stayed here, waiting.

Then she changed her mind. She would not wait any longer. She called our father, bought airplane tickets, rented a car. What would have happened if Parvati had called, had forgiven her? Would she have gone back and would we have stayed there, like Renee, like Sati, never seeing our family outside again? Would the outside world begin to seem too foreign, too faraway, to rejoin? Eventually, I wondered, would I have believed? I imagined myself older, serving Parvati, being punished by her, loving her meekly.

The handle on the door turned. Then there was a knock.

"Who is it?"

"It's us," my mother said. "Hello?" She knocked again, more loudly this time. I opened the door. She was holding a paper bag of food. She carried it to the table and the room filled up with the smell of it.

"What did you get?"

"All sorts of things," Eden said. He opened the paper bag on the table and took out three sandwiches wrapped in white wax paper: grilled cheese and tomato with pickles on the side. The sandwiches were warm, the cheese melting down the side. He took out two red-and-white checked paper baskets overflowing with French fries, two cups of vegetable soup with packets of crackers, and two chocolate milkshakes in tall waxy cups.

My mother brought me ice in a plastic cup and a small packet of aspirin. She wrapped the ice in an old T-shirt and told me to hold it to my head.

She touched my bruise gently with her hand. The chip I had
seen in her eye, the missing flower on the blue and white plate. The
piece we had searched for on the kitchen floor, but never found again.

Eden stood in front of the television. He turned it on, and a
line of white opened into a picture of a game show. The sound of
laughter in the background, an announcer in a brown suit. He turned
the knob, looking through the channels.

I sat down in the chair at the table.

Now on the ashram, darshan would be ending, Jaya's baptism
completed, the baby passed around the room, I thought of Sati
parading with Jaya in her long white dress. After we left, I knew
Parvati's devotees would feel more complete, the string that bound
them pulled tighter. They had stayed, they would tell themselves,
while we had lost our way.

I wanted to be there for one more day, to say good-bye, to
know I was doing everything for the last time. I had hoped Sati would
come back to me, that she still loved me. I believed what we had
couldn't fade so quickly, this was only a test of our friendship, and
one day we would lie together in the bed in her parents' house again,
laughing about our only fight.

Now that we were here, in the motel room, I knew this would
not happen. I knew I would think about Sati for the rest of my life
but never see her again.

Eden stared at the television as he ate. The light and shadows
reflecting on his face. On the screen two men rode down the highway on motorcycles. At the window, I pulled the curtain slightly
apart. The man was gone. His car was gone too.

We left the motel in the morning. In the diner, our mother looked
into her beige-colored cup of tea. "Why can't they ever get it right?
The Americans simply cannot make a cup of tea, the water's never
boiling. They pour the water and milk and then put the tea bag in."

In London, this would be what she told people about America. As though the watery beige cup of tea was what she would remember. Maybe it was the easiest, the funniest thing to tell. How would she explain the ashram?

How would I? I imagined telling the girls in my school, their questioning faces. What we would say to our father, to our grandfather? I thought it would be better not to tell him anything, to simply say we were in California. I invented a house near the beach, riding bicycles, roller-skating in the sun, while Eden and I sipped our orange juice with ice and finished our pancakes.

We drove to the airport on winding cliff roads overlooking the ocean and then on a four-lane highway.

"Mum?" Eden said, calling from the backseat.

"Yes?" Mum glanced at him in the rearview mirror.

"Does Dad know we're coming home today?"

"Well, we won't arrive until tomorrow, really."

"Is he happy?"

I saw her still face, in the mirror.

"Oh, of course he is," she said. "He can't wait to see you."

I looked out the window. A long truck passed on our right. A woman in sunglasses drove a convertible. She was not telling him a lie; she was not telling him the truth. She was telling him what he wanted to believe. She was shaping the world around him, smoothing away the edges, so that when he was older he would not remember this moment: sitting in the backseat of a car on the way to the airport, going home to a father who had not tried to find us.

I imagined our mother phoning our father collect from the motel room, asking for money. "Why should I pay for the tickets? Why should I give you money for kids I never see? We had a nice life here, Lucy. You took them away from me."

Eden turned, looking at me. His face full, a smile on his lips. The knot in the balloon tied, the air sealed inside. The road full of long trucks, of shining cars. The blue sky, the airplanes flying low, flying higher and disappearing into the sky.

In the airport shop, Eden held a snow globe in his hand. Inside, a surfer rode a large blue wave. I turned the rack of postcards: the Hollywood sign, beaches—places we had never been. Roller skaters on the boardwalk, hand prints in the pavement—a California we hadn't seen. I bought the postcards to show the girls at my school. Along the wall hung black T-shirts with CALIFORNIA written in sparkly gold letters.

As we walked through the terminal, I imagined I heard Parvati's voice through the sound of the crowd and the engines of the planes outside: *What are you going home to? Fights and unhappiness?*

Our mother held the tickets in her hand. She stood with Eden looking through the glass walls at the airplanes outside. The sun fell against her skin, the lines in her forehead visible in the light. She touched the glass with her hand and drew an invisible line, watching her finger travel down. Eden stood beside her, his face pressed close to the glass.

Outside, the planes landed in the sun, rolling down the long dark runway. The roaring sound of their motors came through the airport walls. Announcements played on the loudspeakers, and we lined up for our flight.

At the British Airways terminal, the English were returning home, tanned or sunburned from their holidays. Boarding the plane in socks and sandals. Two children wore Mickey Mouse caps with plastic ears. We stood behind an old woman who told us she was from Leeds. She had come to California to visit her granddaughters. She held a bag of English sweets, blackberry with licorice centers, and offered one to each of us.

TWENTY-FOUR

The day was just beginning as we landed at Heathrow. Outside the airport windows, the sky looked overcast, gray. A friendly customs official whistled while he checked our passports, pressing down the stamp. "Welcome home," he said.

Our mother looked anxiously through the crowd of people who had come to meet the arrivals. We stared at the waiting crowd, looking for him, and saw our father standing beside a man holding a taxi sign. He stood with his arms crossed and his eyes looked heavy, tired as he checked his wristwatch.

"Simon!" our mother called out. His eyes crossed the crowd but did not seem to see us.

"Dad!" Eden waved.

We stood together as he made his way toward us.

"Hello, darlings," he said, opening his arms. He hugged Eden and me tightly.

"Hello, Simon," I heard our mother say, as she stood behind us.

"Hello, Lucy." They kissed each other on the cheek. He touched her lightly on the shoulder and then pulled away. I saw him look down at her denim skirt and gray sweater tied with a belt around her waist. Her hair was pulled back, brushed smoothly. In the fluorescent light, from the side, I could see that she had put on lipstick.

"Look at you," he said to me. "Your hair is so blonde." I smiled at him, nervously.

"You've gotten so thin," our father said to Eden. "I would have hardly recognized you. Didn't they feed you there?"

"I didn't like the food," Eden said.

"Well, I'll make you a good breakfast when we get home."

"We better get our luggage," our mother said. "I can see them queuing at the carousel."

Outside, the damp smell of the rain mixed with the city air. Our father pushed the luggage cart across the lot to the car.

Inside, the early morning news played on the car radio and my father held his hands tightly around the steering wheel as we drove away from the airport. The gray sky fell, like a lowered hand, over the rows of houses. The shopkeepers were just opening their doors, turning the lights on inside.

"Was the flight okay?" our father asked, looking at Eden and me in the rearview mirror.

"It was long." I squeezed my hands together in my lap. I felt frozen. Whenever we were apart and came back together, it took me some time to feel comfortable around him again.

"Did you sleep?"

"A little."

"Was the film good?"

Our mother looked out of the passenger-side window. There were only a few other cars on the road, and the windows of the houses were still dark.

"It was all right," I said.

"I liked it," Eden said.

As we drove down Wondle Road, the green door of our house stood like a person who had come to greet us. On the street, a man in a business suit walked a white and brown Jack Russell on a lead, as he read the morning paper. Our father parked the car and carried the luggage from the boot. I held the handle of the door but did not want to get out of the car. I watched my mother and Eden follow my father up the steps of our house.

I saw them look back at me and I opened the car door. The air was damp and the wind blew softly down our street. It was the end of February, and we stood on the doorstep in our summer clothes and cardigans.

"It's like Fort Knox trying to unlock the door," our father said, looking at his ring of keys. I had to change the locks and put in a dead bolt. The house next door was burgled twice. The thieves stuck a wire up the mail chute, unlocking it from the inside. I have to say, they're bloody smart, aren't they. If only they'd put their minds to good use."

Our mother picked up the bottle of milk left on the doorstep. Except for the man walking his dog, there was no one outside. I imagined that, in a moment, the doors of all the houses on our street would open and our neighbors would come out to say hello to us.

Our father turned the final lock and opened the door. I felt my heart beating quickly. I looked at Eden and at Mum, unsure of who would walk in first.

"Well, go on, one of you," our father said. "I can't hold the door all day."

Our mother walked inside. She switched on the hall light, looking at the stairs and the floor. She touched her hand to the wall as she walked cautiously. I saw her turn to look at herself in the hall mirror. She touched the post on the table and then took her hand away.

I took a breath. This was the scent of our house. I breathed in deeply, trying to capture it. Trying to name it.

Porridge peered from the side of the stairway, her tail twitching. "Porridge," Eden called, as he walked toward her, but she turned away. Slowly she appeared from around the stairs and came toward him, letting him scratch her cheeks. When I knelt down and stroked her back, a handful of fur came off in my hand.

"Are you hungry?" our father asked, as we followed him into the kitchen. "Why don't I make us a good breakfast?" He rubbed his hands together standing in his charcoal suit.

We watched him as he took the eggs and sausages from the refrigerator.

"So what did you do there, on the ashram?" our father asked us.

I looked at Eden and Eden looked at me. I saw out mother stroking Porridge in the hallway. Behind the kitchen sink sat a striped blue and white bowl and a green vase in the shape of a fish. For as long as I could remember, the bowl and the vase had been there.

"We went to school. And there was a pond and we went swimming so much, sometimes five or six times in one day. I could swim the whole length and back."

"Did you like it there?"

"I have a best friend now," Eden said. "His name's Jabe and we built a fort in the grapefruit grove."

"Grapefruits? I bet they were delicious there."

"They were," Eden said.

"What about you, darling?" my father asked me.

"I became friends with a girl name Sati." I thought just by saying her name he would see her; he would know all about her.

Our mother walked into the kitchen. She looked around at the things inside, as though seeing them for the first time. In place of the wooden table that Porridge had used as a scratching post was a modern table with stainless steel legs.

"You took down the painting of the people at the beach," she said.

"It's at the framer's," our father said to her.

She touched the tabletop and then walked to the garden doors, where she stood looking out through the square glass panes. Then she turned and walked back to the table. She pulled out a chair and sat down quietly, as though she were a visitor.

"Tea?" our father said.

"Yes, please," Mum said, rubbing her eyes.

He poured her a cup and carried it over, placing it on the table before her. She watched the steam rise into the air, then lifted the cup to her lips.

"I haven't had a decent cup since we left. The Americans cannot make a cup of tea to save their lives."

He laughed, slightly, but there was something else settling into his face. He turned to the stove, taking down the large frying pan from the rack, cutting a piece of butter.

"Lucy," he said, "I went to India on business, and when I came back all of you were gone and there was a note on the table for me."

My mother put both hands around her cup of tea.

"I don't understand why you left. I really don't. You knew I'd be back in a week or two. It's not fair anymore."

"We wanted to get away too," she said, but she did not look at him. "I never expected to stay this long, it just happened."

"It just happened? Do you ever think about anybody else?"

She looked at him angrily.

"How do you think I felt, coming home again to this empty house?" He touched the handle of the frying pan, watching the butter melt, waiting for an answer.

"We spoke about this on the telephone," she said.

"Lucy, I hardly recognized your voice when you phoned from California. You sounded like someone else."

"It was probably the connection," she said. She held the tea steady in her hands, the expression on her face blank and aloof.

"Are you enlightened now? Or happy, finally?" Our father did not raise his voice, but it was as though small stones were spitting from his mouth.

The tea spilled over the sides of our mother's cup as she lowered it to the saucer. She sat looking at her hands on the table. On her left hand she still wore her rose-gold wedding band.

He had broken the eggs in the blue-and-white bowl, added milk, salt, and pepper. He fried the toast in the pan and cut the tomato and mushrooms in half.

In the morning light, her eyes looked tired and her skin dry like paper. "Breakfast won't be ready for at least fifteen minutes, why don't you two take your cases up to your rooms," our father said. His back was turned to us.

I was afraid to leave the kitchen. In the past, when they had been apart and came back together, my father would stare at my mother as if she were the only person in the room, the only window with a view. Since we arrived this morning, they had hardly looked at each other.

Eden ran ahead of me, up the stairs to his room. He opened the door but stopped inside, looking around.

"What is it?" I said.

"My model airplanes and army tanks," he said.

They were not on the top of the chest of drawers where he had left them. There was a glass of water and an ashtray. The bedsheets had been pulled up messily, and in the corner were a guitar, men's jeans, and a pair of shoes. I recognized the guitar as belonging to a friend of our father's named Clovis, who spent most of the year in India and stayed at his friends' houses when he came back to town.

Eden turned in a circle in the small room. He opened the cupboard door and found his models in a box, piled together. He sat down on the bed, taking out one at a time, making sure they were not broken.

My bedroom seemed the same as I had left it. I walked over to the painted chest of drawers with the wooden hairbrush and bowl of odd hair clips and elastic bands. I opened one of the drawers and took out a pale green shirt that had been one of my favorites. It smelled faintly of washing soap.

I sat down on the bottom bunk, looking at the porthole window. I was back in my bedroom. I thought of the bridge I had imagined the first day in California, a bridge that connected us through the sky. From the window I could see the tops of the houses across the street: windows and chimneys.

I opened the doors of my wardrobe, looking at the clothes on the hangers. I still had the navy dress my grandmother from America bought me when she came to visit and took me to the ballet. I held it against me; I had the feeling I should dress up for the day. I put it on and pulled the zipper up the back. When I looked in the mirror it looked as though my arms were too long, hanging down from the satin cuffs of the dress. It was too tight across my chest.

There used to be an old lady down the road who dressed like a young girl. She wore plaits with ribbons in her hair and red rouge painted in circles on her cheeks. I reminded myself of her. I brushed my hair, stepping closer to the mirror, just looking. Then I unzipped the dress and put it back on the hanger.

As I was closing the wardrobe door, I saw a cloth bag made of floral pattern fabric. The women in Sloane Square who wore capri trousers and ballerina flats carried these bags. They looked as though they were for toiletries, but they used them as handbags and overnight cases.

Inside the bag were clothes. I pulled out what I thought was a blouse, but when I held it up I could see that it was a dress for a little girl, a white eyelet dress for a three- or four-year-old. I looked at it, wondering if it had belonged to me when I was young, but I knew that it hadn't.

From the bedroom window I could see the city street below, the tops of cars, and the people walking quickly as though they were gliding on ice. A pigeon landed on a windowsill, then flew away. I thought, If I stand here long enough, I'll see the children coming home from school, the people coming home from work, the lights going on in the houses, and the lights going off again.

I wondered what Sati was doing now and the other girls on the ashram: dressing for darshan, running across the grass in the night, working in the stables with Valerie. I hoped Sati missed me, the way I missed her. I said a prayer that she did. I wanted to take a photograph of myself, of my bedroom, of the front of our house, and send it to her. I wanted her to know where I lived.

I imagined the things Sati and Valerie would do together. I wondered if Sati would invite her to sleep over, in the loft bed, and spell words with her finger on her back. Would she write the words *I love you*? I shook my head. "No," I said, alone in my room. No, she would not write *I love you* on her back. That was something Sati would only say to me.

I had taken the clothes she had lent me to wear to kids' night with Parvati and never returned them. They were in my suitcase, the blouse and the dark tight jeans. I thought I would put them on, brush my hair, and walk down the street in them. I would walk to my old school and stand outside the gates, waiting for the girls in my form to notice me. But as I unzipped the suitcase, I imagined Samantha Fenton and Sheba Marks giggling, laughing at me in my too-tight jeans.

"May?" I heard my father's voice at the door. "Didn't you hear me?" he said. "I've been calling your name."

He walked into the room and I stood up, leaving the open suitcase on the floor.

"Breakfast is ready."

"Thanks."

"I'm glad you're back. I missed you and your brother."

The light from the window fell in an oval against the floor. Outside, the day had brightened. We could hear the sound of the traffic on the street below.

"Dad?"

"Yes?"

"Why didn't you try to phone us? Or come to see us in California?"

My father looked away with a sigh. "Your mother's the one who took you away. She only phoned me once the whole time, to tell me she wasn't coming home."

There was an expression on his face. A grimness, as though he had come to a decision he did not want to make.

"Did your mother tell you that she gave the guru three thousand pounds? Those were her Marks & Spencer shares her father gave her when she turned eighteen. They would have been yours someday."

"Mum's never cared about money," I said

"Everyone cares about money, darling. You'll realize that when you have to take care of yourself."

"You had a guru once," I said.

"Maharaji was a fat man in a bedsheet. A little less flash than this one." My father held his hand out to me. "Come on," he said. "Breakfast will be getting cold."

In the kitchen, the table was set. Our father brought the scrambled eggs to the table in the frying pan, spooning them out on each plate with fried toast, sausages, fried mushrooms, and tomatoes. I ate the eggs, bread, and tomatoes but I hadn't eaten meat since we left London, and the sausages looked gray and unappealing.

Our father glanced at his wristwatch, a gift from *his* father, who had won it in a bet. He turned the small windup dial.

"I really tried to take the day off, but I have an important client, a collector, coming round the shop at ten," he said. "We're thinking of going into business together. Maybe opening a second shop on Draycott Avenue." His voice sounded strained, rehearsed, as though he were building himself up for us.

On the table stood the glass vase that opened like a flower. He took a last sip of his coffee and put the cup down on the table. He stood up, brushing down the front of his trousers.

"All right. I better be off."

He walked to my side and put his arm around me, kissing me on the check. He kissed Eden and then he said good-bye to our mother.

"I'll come back after the meeting," he said. "We'll do something nice together this afternoon."

Our mother stood up. She followed him to the front door.

Eden and I sat at the kitchen table in silence but could not hear what they were saying. The front door closed, and after a moment our mother walked into the kitchen. She pulled her hair away from her face, tying it with the elastic on her wrist.

Eden took the bottle cap from the milk and gave it to Porridge to lick the cream from.

"Don't do that, Eden, you know he hates that," Mum said.

"Who?"

"Your father."

"But he's not here."

Mum put her teacup down. She walked over to the garden doors and stood looking out. She held her cardigan around her. She leaned her forehead against the window glass.

We could not see her face, only the back of her, the arch of her neck. She looked as though she was shivering and then I realized that she was crying.

Eden and I stayed at the table, watching her cry.

As we sat there, I remembered something my mother had told me. When she was a young girl, when she was upset and when she cried, her mother had never tried to comfort her. She had longed for her mother to put her arms around her, but she could only offer a tissue or a pat on the shoulder.

Our mother's crying grew louder. She tried the handle on the door, to let herself out, but a new lock had been put in and as she pushed the handle it rattled the glass but would not open.

I thought I should go to her. I should comfort her, the way Sati had comforted her mother. I put my hands on the chair to push myself up but felt unable to move. It was as though I were made of stone.

Eden walked slowly toward her. "Mum?" he said. "Mum, why are you crying?" When he was near her she reached for him, pulling him close. Her crying calmed as she held him to her. When she lifted her head, her face was wet with tears. Eden stood beside her, his arm around her waist. She tried to catch her breath. Her nose ran like a child's, and she wiped it with the back of her hand.

She shook her head, taking a breath. "I'm sorry," she said. "I don't know what I'm doing with our lives." She wiped her eyes with her cardigan sleeve. "I feel completely lost," she said, as though she were surrendering, laying down the cards.

It was a quarter to ten in the morning.

I stood up and walked to the garden doors. I stood next to her, but I could not put my arm around her.

She wiped her eyes and turned, looking at the clock. "It's so early," she said. "I'm going to lie down for a bit." She walked to the sink and poured a glass of water, drinking it as she stood, leaning one hand against the counter.

Our mother went upstairs to the bedroom, Eden went to watch the telly in the sitting room, but it was ten in the morning and the cartoons were over. Eden said he was going to go upstairs to his room, and I sat on the sofa watching a cooking show.

An advert came on for no-tangle shampoo and conditioner. There was a girl in the bath washing her hair, with a head full of bubbles. I thought there was something familiar about her. Then, on the television, she was walking through the park with her hair flowing, straight, shiny, and blonde.

It was Greta. I stepped closer to the screen, but the advert was already ending. Greta smiled at the camera. There was something different about her; her teeth were whiter.

I turned away from the television. I thought about the night she had made me take my boots on and off, the rain boots that had scraped a blister on my heel, and now she was on television. When I had told Sati about Greta, she had said that she would have bad karma. That she would never be on television, and everyone will see how mean she is. But Sati was wrong. On television Greta looked pretty and friendly, smiling with her white teeth.

I turned off the television and went upstairs.

I stood in the doorway of Eden's room, watching him play. He had taken his Legos and metal trains and army figures from the cupboard and arranged them in a circle around himself on the floor. Then he repositioned an army figure, moving it so he stood on top of the Lego wall.

"What time is Dad coming back?" Eden asked.

"I don't know. He said this afternoon."

Eden looked at the circle of toys around him, staring into it as though he were staring into another world. I lay down on the single bed, turning my head into the pillow. I closed my eyes, listening to Eden and the low hissing of the radiator.

Later, I went to the kitchen and washed the breakfast dishes left on the table.

I squeezed the green fairy liquid into the sink of hot water. When they were clean I laid the dishes on a tea towel to dry. I scrubbed the frying pan, and wiped the counters. I thought, My father will be happy to see the kitchen clean when he comes home.

The telephone rang and I went to answer it.

"Hello?" a woman said, but she sounded unsure.

I waited a moment, wrapping my fingers around the cord. I could see myself in the doors.

"Is Simon there?"

I held the phone to my ear. "I'm sorry," I said, "he's not in right now. Can I take a message?"

I thought I could hear a child's voice in the background. "That's all right. I'll try him later," she said, and hung up.

I stood by the phone, listening to the dial tone. Then I put the receiver down. I stood in the kitchen, listening to the clock tick on the wall behind me and thinking of the sound of the woman's voice, like a gold chain.

I went outside to the garden. I watched Porridge walking alongside the wall, stepping through the plants and flowerpots. The air was damp but not cold. Porridge circled the terrapin pond. Twigs and brown leaves floated on the water, but the terrapin was nowhere to be seen. From the garden the lights in the kitchen shone softly, warm and yellow.

TWENTY-FIVE

In the afternoon, our father came home. He hung his coat on the rack and left his keys on the table beneath the mirror. Our mother had taken a nap and a bath. She sat in the kitchen, dressed in a brown sweater and jeans, her hair still damp against her back.

The kettle boiled on the stove behind her.

"Did you rest?" our father asked, looking at her.

"A bit."

"You look better," he said.

The kettle whistled and she stood up, pouring water into the teapot. "How was your meeting?"

My father nodded. "Quite good, actually. Looks like it's a go."

My mother held her hand on the handle of the kettle. "Great," she said.

She brought the pot to the table and four cups, pouring tea for each of us.

"I spoke to my father," she said. "When I phoned, Mrs. Stirling answered and told me he hadn't been well. He didn't say anything to me about not feeling well, but he asked me to bring him peaches. He's never asked me to bring him anything before."

There was an expression on my father's face, as though he were holding his breath.

"I told him we'd come up this weekend."

"We're going to Scotland?" I said.

Eden looked from our mother to our father. "Dad, are you coming too?"

Our mother looked at Eden but no one answered him.

"How will you explain this to him?" our father asked.

"Explain what?"

"The ashram, being away for so long."

She shook her head. "I don't know what I'll say."

"Mum, are we going to stay for long?" Eden asked.

"Maybe until my father's feeling well again."

Our father nodded. "Then what will you do?"

"I don't know, Simon."

She laughed, lightly, like a bird released from a hand.

Our father looked away from her; his eyes went to the garden doors. "It's not too cold today," he said. He brought his thumb and forefinger to the bridge of his nose. "Anyone phone while I was out?"

I shook my head. "No one phoned," I said.

When we finished our tea we went for a walk. We dressed in our coats and hats and put on our winter shoes. Eden's shoes did not fit at all and mine were tight in the toes.

"First thing we're going to do," our father said, as he locked the front door, "is go to the shoe shop and buy this boy a new pair of shoes."

"Trainers, Dad," Eden said. "Can I have trainers?"

"Whatever you want," he said, as he put his keys in the pocket of his navy coat and walked down the front steps.

On the street we passed our neighbor Claire walking with her five-year-old twins. I had seen these children since they were small, every weekday the same routine: the brother and sister dressed alike walking with their mother or with their nanny.

"Well, hello," Claire said. "I haven't seen you for ages."

"We were in America," my mother said. "California."

"California, how nice," she said touching her hairband on her head. "Wonderful weather."

She looked at my mother intensely as though searching for something beyond her face. "You look nice and tan."

I felt myself smiling stiffly at her. The mother was older than our mother, but her children were still young. She had straight brown hair cut to her shoulders; she wore a raincoat, straight trousers that went to her calves, and flat shoes without socks.

"Well, welcome back," she said, "I have to get the children to their French tutor."

I remembered now, as we watched her hail a taxi, that I had had the impression she didn't approve of us. That she had seen us leaving the house with suitcases and that she had heard my mother and father fighting on the street at night.

On the High Street, people walked past in a hurry, carrying shopping bags. A group of schoolchildren crossed the road, dressed in matching uniforms. Two teenagers kissed at the bus stop. The boy had purple hair and wore black boots to his knees. A woman stood outside the newsagent's, smoking a cigarette.

We walked in the direction of the park. The air was cool and the sky overcast.

We waited at the street for the light to change; two red buses went by in a row. At the corner, a mother and her daughter stood waiting to cross. The girl was wearing a red coat with white tights and patent leather shoes; her hair was tied with a ribbon on the side. Her mother held a wrapped present under her arm. The girl and her mother looked back at us, and I smiled at them, a wide, bright smile. I stepped closer to my father, too afraid to take his hand. I looked at the line of us, Dad, Eden, and Mum. Look, I thought moving my head to the side, as though listening to a song, we're a family.

*   *   *

In the park, Eden said he wanted to go on the swings. "Will you push me, Dad?" Eden yelled from the swing.

"Can't you do it yourself?" he said, fixing the scarf around his neck.

My mother looked over her shoulder at him. They sat next to each other on the bench. "Go on," she said, under her breath.

"Oh, all right. Here I come, Eden," he called through the playground. Eden held the chains of the swing, his feet on the rubber ground beneath him, waiting as our father walked casually toward him.

I sat on the bench with my mother, with the empty space where my father had been between us. We watched Eden on the swing, his hair blowing forward, then back, his cheeks turning rose-colored from the wind. He laughed at something our father was saying.

I looked at Eden. Sometimes, when he slept, the soft baby look of his face was still there, but he was changing; the slope of his nose, the roundness in his face, was leaving him. He was one of the older boys in the playground now.

I remembered that I loved the smell in the park of the grass and leaves and the damp air. Once, Sati and I were lying in the sun by the side of the pond. She had her eyes closed and she said, "Describe London to me."

Dear Sati, I thought,

This is what London feels like: like looking at the city through a very fine gauze. So that it is a city, but everything is softer. In California things shone in the sun; here, everything is misted. That's why it's beautiful. I would have never noticed if we had not been away and come back.

I felt my mother looking at me. "Your bruise is fading," she pushed my hair off my forehead, looking at my bruise. I was sure she knew there was something I wasn't telling her.

I thought of Mum, standing on the dock at the ashram, looking out at Eden and Jabe. "He's so happy," she had said aloud, but she had never asked us if we wanted to stay.

"Look how happy Eden is now," I said. "You never asked us what we wanted, Mum. You never did and you still don't. We just got back and now we're going to Scotland."

"Your grandfather isn't well," she said.

"I know, but you never even phoned him while we were in California."

I thought of us packing the car, driving through London on a Saturday morning, when the streets were quiet and empty. Passing the towns along the way, stopping for lunch at the Little Chef on the hill. Our mother would enroll us in the village school. Then I thought of the boy, Nicholas, standing alone with his hands in his coat pockets outside the dairy wall.

The wind blew through the playground, and she held the neck of her coat closed with her hands. Her face looked tired, cracked in the cool weather.

"I know you're angry with me," she said. "I'm sorry, May. You'll see what it's like when you're a mother. I'm trying my best."

I shook my head. "I'm not angry, Mum."

My mother looked away. A group of young children in school uniforms ran onto the playground, their mothers following behind them, carrying their satchels and talking to one another as they sat on the benches.

Once, in a park in London, I watched a boy—he was six or seven years old—gather flowers for his mother from inside a wrought-iron railing, while she read a newspaper on the bench. The boy collected the flowers carefully, only picking the best ones. He held them together in his hand, a small bouquet for her.

He carried the flowers to his mother, holding them out to her. "These are for you, Mum," the boy had said. She looked at him from over the paper and then glanced around the park, until she saw the place behind the wrought-iron fence where he had picked them.

"Where did you get these flowers?" She took his wrists so tightly the flowers fell from his hands.

He looked at her but couldn't speak.

"You took them from over there," she said angrily, her face close to his. "You're not meant to pick the flowers in the park. They're for everybody to look at."

When she let go of his hands, he stood staring at the place where she had held his wrists. His mother watched him for a moment before taking up the paper beside her. The purple flowers had fallen together, except for a few scattered below the bench.

I thought of that boy. He would be Eden's age by now, the softness of his face leaving him. And I knew that in some way, that day when his mother scolded him for picking the flowers, something in him would have changed toward her, as it would through his life, changing the full, complete love a young child feels for his mother.

We left the park before it was dark and walked home along the High Street. We passed the café whose menu of carry-out food we had looked at in our room in the ashram. The street was busy with people carrying packages from the shops or standing at the bus stops, on their way home from work. We passed the bookstore, the chemist, and the bank. Sale signs were posted in the shop windows and advertisements on the bus.

On the corner, we could see the lights on through the windows of Tiger, Tiger. I saw people inside, but when we were near I realized the windows were bare and the shop inside empty. A sign posted on the door gave the name of the store that would be taking its place, a clothing chain that already had two other shops on the High Street. What I had thought were people inside was only a reflection of the people waiting at the bus stop across the street.

"Oh, Mum," Eden said. "I told Jabe I would send him a present from here."

"Who's Jabe?" our father asked, as he stared into the empty windows of the shop. Inside, in the bare room, were a ladder and paint can.

"He's Eden's friend on the ashram," our mother said.

"Remember, Dad?" Eden looked up at him. "I told you about him this morning."

I looked at my father's reflection in the shop window. We would live apart, and there would be pieces of each other's lives we would never know. We continued down the High Street; the sky was dark blue and the yellow streetlights shone against it.

"Maybe we'll go round to the Indian for dinner if you're not too tired," our father said. "On second thought, I've got some delicious olive oil that Rafael brought me back from his farm in Italy. Maybe I'll make pasta. Would you like that?"

"That sounds good, Simon," I heard our mother say.

"Let me just pop into Ian's and pick up a bottle of wine," he said.

Mum, Eden, and I waited outside on the pavement in front of the wineshop. Mum looked into the window, decorated with wooden crates and bottles of wine and champagne. A double-decker bus went by and three girls my age jumped off, laughing and holding hands as they ran up the street.

Dad came from the shop, the narrow paper bag in his hand. "Got a nice bottle of Chianti," he said.

My mother smiled, a smile that seemed too weak to hold on her face. A smile that lived for one heartbeat.

There was firmness in my father's voice, quickness in his step. He stopped on the corner, buttoning the top button of his coat, as though he were closing himself against her.

"Dad?" Eden said. "What are we having for pudding?"

"I'll tell you what," he said, taking his money clip from his pocket. "Why don't you two run over to Raj and pick up some ice cream, and your Mum and I will get dinner started." He leafed through the bills, pulled out a five-pound note, and handed it to Eden.

"Thanks, Dad." Eden held the bill between his hands.

"Loseley's," our father said. "It's the best."

Eden put the five-pound note in his pocket as we turned the corner to the market.

In the shop we walked the aisles to the freezer, looking through the glass at the boxes of ice cream. We found the Loseley's chocolate and vanilla that said, "made with Devon milk" on the box and took it to the register. An Indian woman stood behind the cash register. She held the five-pound note up to the light, looking at the watermark.

We carried the ice cream down the street to our house. The lights were on in the kitchen, and we could see inside. We saw our mother and father making dinner. She opened a cupboard door while he filled a pot of water at the sink. Our mother set the table. The bottle of red wine stood on the counter.

Eden and I stood outside our house in the night, watching them. I imagined us walking along the hallway to the kitchen. We would sit down at the table together: father, mother, daughter, and son. And if someone, anyone—a stranger—walking down our street tonight looked into our windows, they would see a family sitting down to dinner.

Why was this so hard for us? In Scotland my grandfather would say to her, Why would you give all this up, to live with the gypsies, to live on an ashram? And our mother would look at him, startled, as though she had never thought that she was giving anything up. As though she had only thought she would be gaining more.

Through the window, I saw my father say something to her. They were not standing far apart, but he reached out to her. He put his hand on her arm, pulling her close to him. When she was near, he wrapped both arms around her and she leaned her face against the side of his neck.

I remembered a day in the park, skipping behind my mother and father, telling Eden to skip beside me.

"Skip with me!" I told him, as our parents walked ahead, arguing.

The tap of our shoes on the pavement, the bounce of trees and grass, pretending to everyone who walked by—to the man sitting on the park bench, to the children playing on the sloping lawn—that we were a happy family.

Eden walked up the steps, the bag of ice cream in his hand.

"May?" he said, turning back to look at me. "Are you coming?"

A man on the street walked his dog. He held the evening newspaper beneath his arm. Two people stood talking at the bus stop. The woman held her coat around her with her hands. The man looked away, his hands in the pockets of his suit jacket.

Eden stood outside the green door. The lights were on in the houses across the street. I looked at the billowing shapes of curtains, at the people inside moving from room to room. The glow of yellow lights, as though a fire were burning inside.

ACKNOWLEDGMENTS

I would like to thank my editor Elisabeth Schmitz for refining and focusing the story and the writing.

My agent Kim Witherspoon for her sound and wise advice.

Anna Van Lenten for reading drafts and generously offering good advice.

Sam Brumbaugh for his support and encouragement while I was writing this book.

Once again I am so happy to be part of the Grove/Atlantic family and want to thank Morgan Entrekin, Deb Seager, Charles Woods, Gretchen Mergenthaler, Michael Hornburg, and Jessica Monahan.

My family: Jett Craze, Sophy Craze, Polly Smith, Edward Craze, Victoria Craze, Carol Shiff . . . Thank you. India. Rowan and Tess xoxo.